# MOTHER EARTH'S TEARS

## L.M. Henderson

**BALBOA**
PRESS

A DIVISION OF HAY HOUSE

Balboa Press books may be ordered through booksellers or by contacting:

Balboa Press
A Division of Hay House
1663 Liberty Drive
Bloomington, IN 47403
www.balboapress.com
1-(877) 407-4847

ISBN: 978-1-4525-5974-2
ISBN: 978-1-4525-5975-9

Because of the dynamic nature of the Internet, any web addresses or
links contained in this book may have changed since publication and
may no longer be valid. The views expressed in this work are solely those
of the author and do not necessarily reflect the views of the publisher,
and the publisher hereby disclaims any responsibility for them.

The author of this book does not dispense medical advice or prescribe the use
of any technique as a form of treatment for physical, emotional, or medical
problems without the advice of a physician, either directly or indirectly. The
intent of the author is only to offer information of a general nature to help
you in your quest for emotional and spiritual well-being. In the event you use
any of the information in this book for yourself, which is your constitutional
right, the author and the publisher assume no responsibility for your actions.

Any people depicted in stock imagery provided by Thinkstock are models,
and such images are being used for illustrative purposes only.
Certain stock imagery © Thinkstock.
Printed in the United States of America
Balboa Press rev. date: 10/02/2012

*I dedicate this book to my family and friends
who are always encouraging me*

# INTRODUCTION

The Olympic Peninsula in Washington State is beautiful. I have a friend who lives there, and every year when I visit her I find more and more things to learn and like about it. I became inspired to write this book the last two times I visited. The land isn't crowded with building and malls, and the wild life is happy it can move around freely and enjoy their life.

There are herds of elk in that part of the world, and they actually look around for a place to rest each night. There are warning lights on the main road, and when they are blinking it means that a herd of elk could be nearby, and that people should drive with caution. Bald eagles nest in the trees growing in this wondrous scenic place. The rivers and lakes throughout the peninsula are a sight to behold.

This book is fiction, but the story could happen anywhere. Enjoy the journey and I guarantee you'll come away with a new understanding and love for this beautiful and vulnerable planet we live on.

# CHAPTER ONE

THE WARRENS HAD LIVED IN this town for about 20 years. Elise, 45, was mother to Meg who graduated from high school this year, and to Scotty who was nine years old. Robert Warren, 50, was their father. The Warrens owned the hardware store in town, and Robert and Elise were busy working there almost all of the time. Once in a while they got their kids to help.

Elise was known for bringing lavish dishes to various events and parties. She also loved canning food. The Warrens grew apples, cherries, and sweet onions on their property. Robert was a hard worker and the hardware store was basically his idea. They opened the store 15 years ago and did a wonderful business there. Everyone in town knew the family. You could buy what you needed for building, painting, and anything else for the home and garden.

The Warren's best friends were the Chapmans. Lottie, 42, was a personal chef for many families in town. Tom Chapman owned a lumber company. Their son, Billy, 16, had another year of high school before graduating. He and Meg Warren were best pals, and have been since they were very small children.

Blissville was a peaceful and beautiful town nestled in the Olympic Peninsula in Washington State. The population was around 5,000 people. Everyone knew each other and there was a friendly atmosphere in the community. However, lately there had been rumors about old Tyrone Blake, 80 years old, wanting to sell his 50 acres to a developer. People were not happy with Tyrone, and they gossiped about it constantly. So far, he hadn't taken any action towards that development. Tyrone was diagnosed with colon cancer recently. This is why he wanted to sell the land and go live with his daughter in Seattle for the duration of his life.

Tyrone inherited this land from his parents, who inherited it from their parents and had been taking care of it and working the fields of corn for years. He also had pigs and chickens to sustain him. He was considered by many to be grumpy and unfriendly, especially to children.

The phone rang and Meg answered it. "Hey Meg, want to go to the river? It's a beautiful day for it," Billy Chapman asked.

"Sounds great, Billy. Let me change clothes. I'll be there in about 15 minutes."

Billy and Meg loved to hike and explore the area where they lived. There were many trails, and small hills to hike and they were always looking for new and fun places to add to their repertoire. Meg's brother, Scotty, loved to go with them when he could convince them to let him come along. Today was no different.

"Where are you and Billy going today?" Scotty asked with a little pout on his face.

"Out."

"Out where?"

"Just out."

"Please Meg. Summer vacations are so boring. I won't bother you guys, honest."

"Scotty, you're such a pest. Okay, get your hiking shoes on and you can come along."

"You're the greatest sister a kid could have," Scotty said with his arms wrapped around Meg's waist.

Meg watched Scotty while their parents were working at the hardware store. She felt obligated to make sure Scotty wasn't alone for long in case he needed something or in case of an emergency.

"Let's go around the river today. I love it there," Billy said to Meg and Scotty.

"I love it there also," Meg answered. "It's so beautiful and peaceful."

"Hey, look guys. I don't remember seeing this trail before. Why am I noticing it now?" Billy asked.

"You weren't very observant," Meg said to Billy.

"Touche," Billy laughed.

"Let's go and see where it leads. I love exploring," Scotty said enthusiastically.

"Hold on, Scotty. Don't run ahead, and don't leave our side. We stick together. Especially when we're going somewhere we haven't been before," Meg warned.

"She's right, Scotty. Stick close and we'll find out together where this trail leads," Billy agreed.

# CHAPTER TWO

M EG, SCOTTY, AND BILLY SAT down on a big rock to have a snack before exploring any further. Meg and Billy were discussing what college Meg was thinking of going to. She had decided to just take it easy after graduation and use the time to think about what she wanted to do with her life before committing to anything.

"I'm not sure what I want to do, Billy. It's hard making a decision that will influence the rest of my life. Just wait until you have to do it. You'll be graduating next year and I hope you know what you're going to do. The economy is in such a turmoil now, and it's hard finding work. I don't know, I don't want to think about it right now. Let's just have fun."

"I'm hungry Meg," Scotty said. Did you bring any of those Granola bars?"

"I sure did. Do you want one Billy?" Meg said, as she reached into her backpack.

The three of them ate their Granola bars and drank bottled water and talked about the scenery around them. As they were chatting, Scotty stopped talking and told Meg and

Billy to stop also. He was listening very intently at something that caught his attention.

"Do you guys hear that?" Scotty said excitedly.

"Hear what?" Billy said munching on his Granola bar.

"Wait, stop eating and listen," Meg said as she got up and walked towards where the sound was coming from.

"You're right. I do hear something. It sounds like gurgling water. Is there a pond or waterfall near here?" Billy inquired.

"Not that I know of," Meg answered.

"Let's go and find out what it is," Scotty suggested anxiously.

"It sounds like it's coming from over there," Meg said, pointing straight ahead of them.

There were three different paths to take in the vicinity where they had stopped. The middle path was where they started to walk to find the source of the water. This path led to just inside of Tyrone's property line. There were no fences, just a grove of Ponderosa pines along the border. Scotty started running ahead of Meg and Billy, and was determined to find something exciting.

"Scotty! Stop! Stay with us, don't run off," Meg warned.

Scotty didn't pay any attention to Meg. He was too keyed up to stop.

"Billy, we have to hurry. I don't want to lose Scotty. There are a lot of places to get lost around here."

Off in the distance, they could hear Scotty yelling at them.

"Hey guys. Come here quick. This is so cool," Scotty shouted.

Meg and Billy were out of breath, and they came to where Scotty was stooping down. He was playing with the water that was bubbling up from the ground. The water was as clear as glass and warm to the touch. There were trees all around and the birds were chirping loudly. It was a beautiful spot, and one they didn't know about.

"I've never seen this place," Meg said astonished.

"I haven't either," Billy agreed.

"You have a good ear, Scotty. I wonder if you're the first one to discover this place. I hope we can find our way back. We're far away from the river," Billy said, worriedly.

"Well, since Scotty is so good at finding things, he can lead us back to where we came from. Right, Scotty?" Meg asked, with her hand on her hip.

"Feel the water you guys, it's warm. It's weird, isn't it? I mean Elkwa River is freezing cold, and the snow melts off the mountains and all the water in the area is really cold. But not this water. I mean, where's the water coming from?" Scotty said, puzzled and excited at the same time.

"I think we should be heading back. Come on guys, we'll come back here again and explore some more. Don't tell anyone about this. Let it be our secret for now, okay?" Meg asked.

"I agree. This is so cool and I don't want a whole bunch of people coming here and ruining this beautiful spot. Do you agree Scotty?" Billy commented.

"Sure. After all, I found it and I don't want people to come here either."

Scotty led Meg and Billy out of the area and got them on the right path to come back to where they started. They got home just in time for dinner.

"Did you guys have fun at the river today?" Elise asked Meg and Scotty.

"Yeah, we did. What's for dinner?" Scotty asked, trying not to tell too much.

"You never have much to say, do you Scotty?" Elise laughed.

Scotty turned red from embarrassment, and went to his room waiting for dinner to be ready.

"How about you, Meg? How was the river today?" Elise attempted to ask again.

"Great, Mom. Where's dad tonight? Still working at the hardware store?"

Elise stood with hands on her hips and shook her head. Meg went up to her room in a hurry.

Robert Warren worked hard at the hardware store. He was finishing up and straightening the counters and closing for the night. He couldn't wait to get home and have a good home cooked meal. Elise worked at the store also, but she always left early each day so she could come home and fix a meal for everyone in the family. This also allowed her the time to pay bills, shop, and do other things that she wouldn't be able to do if she worked all day in the store.

"Hi honey. You look tired. Would you like a glass of wine?" Elise offered her husband.

"Sounds great. It was a busy day today. Old Tyrone came in wanting some paint. We got to talking about him selling his 50 acres to a developer. The conversation got a little heated and several people joined in and gave their opinion. He got angry and left in a huff. That old man doesn't even see what he's doing to this community by selling to that builder."

"Maybe he just doesn't care, Robert. He's dying and he wants to settle things before leaving this earth. I know it's not what we want, but maybe if people weren't so mean to him about it, he would listen."

"I doubt it honey. He has his mind set on it. The developer is coming in another three weeks to talk details with him and get a closer look at the property and surrounding areas."

"Well, dinner is ready. I fried chicken, and we have smashed potatoes and peas. Does that sound good?" Elise asked.

"Sounds wonderful. I love comfort food and I think we could all use some of that right about now."

"Meg, Scotty, dinner's ready," Elise called from downstairs.

# CHAPTER THREE

TYRONE BLAKE WAS HAPPILY MARRIED to Monica Olsen for 50 years. She was 75 when she crossed over from ovarian cancer. This was five years ago. Tyrone never got over the loss. They were active in the community and showed up at all the potlucks and events that went on in Blissville. They were well-liked by everyone. Both Tyrone and Monica worked hard on their property. As they got older it became more difficult to keep it up. Weeds were overtaking the acreage. Their house was a beautifully kept up Victorian style home, but when Monica became sick Tyrone spent all of his time taking care of her. The house was in need of repair, and the land needed attention.

Tyrone found out a year ago that he had colon cancer and didn't want to treat it. He wanted to live it out and stay with his daughter in Seattle until he was ready to leave and be with his wife in the afterlife.

About two months ago, a land developer named James Ackerman approached Tyrone and talked him into selling his property to James' company, Ackerman Associates. He was offered a good price and without hesitation, Tyrone accepted the deal. There was one thing Tyrone made James promise, and that was that he leave the home standing on the property. It was well over 100 years old and belonged to Tyrone's relatives. He inherited this home and the property surrounding it. James Ackerman accepted this, and promised to refurbish the home and make it an historical landmark. It would be a focal point of the plans Ackerman Associates had envisioned for this beautiful property.

The house had five bedrooms, three bathrooms, also a huge kitchen with an eating area in it and a large dining room and a small living room. However, this whole deal with Ackerman Associates didn't sit well with the community. The last thing they wanted was to have condos, a shopping mall, and cement covering this beautiful land. It would also take away customers from the independent businesses in town. Tyrone wasn't thinking about anyone else, he was just thinking that he couldn't cope with the property or the house any longer. He had to get rid of it.

The edge of the property was about half a mile away from Elkwa River. The river and the immediate surrounding area, was owned by the state of Washington. Not many people owned land that close to the river, but Tyrone's family went back generations when it was possible at the time to own this beautiful property.

# CHAPTER FOUR

James Ackerman was 45 years old, and took over his father's business as a real estate developer 10 years ago. The company was based in Seattle. He had scouts looking around the globe for land to build on. Condos, shopping malls, anchor stores, and theatres were all in the scenario for developing land that they convinced people to sell to them. A lot of their clients were aging people, like Tyrone Blake, who couldn't take care of their property anymore. Others were people who had inherited land from relatives and who didn't live on the property but had this land that they didn't know what to do with. They would rather have the money that Ackerman Associates offered them and be rid of the responsibility of the property.

Ackerman was married to Felicia, and had two kids, a boy and a girl, who were in grade school. He had high blood pressure, and high cholesterol which the doctor had warned him to control more than he had been. He was on medication and he was a perfect candidate for a heart attack. The business he was in created a lot of stress and he had on several occasions said that he wanted to sell the company and retire early. His wife agreed and kept encouraging him to do that.

The latest sale of the Blake property in Blissville, which was nearing the end of negotiations, was pretty much the end of any big sales Ackerman Associates planned to develop. James hadn't told any of the people working for him about his plans yet. He wanted to make sure everything developed as it should with the latest acquisition in Blissville.

The type of work James was in made people angry with him for developing land that the community had coveted and lived in for years. This created a good part of the stress for him. He was a good person and loved people and what they had to offer in their lives, and he also respected them. This was what made his job so difficult and why he needed to get out of it. You might say that this latest deal was his swan song.

James was driving to Blissville and took a good look at the Blake home on the property. He made an appointment with Tyrone Blake and needed to see just how much work was required to refurbish it and what his costs would be. It was a long drive, but a beautiful one with the mountains in the background. He needed the time alone to think. As he walked up to the entrance of the Blake home he was looking around at the property surrounding it. There were beautiful flowers close to the house, and a brick path leading up to the front door. Surrounding the property was a view of the snowcapped mountains and they were breathtaking. He was thinking that he had stepped into paradise with the scenery before him.

Somewhere deep in his mind, he understood why the people of this community protested land development, but he had to do this project to secure the financial future of his family. It was his job. It was bittersweet for him and as he was thinking about it he walked up to the door of the house and rang the bell. Tyrone slowly walked towards the door and opened it.

"Hello Mr. Blake, it's nice to see you. I hope I'm not too early. The drive here was quicker than I anticipated."

"Please call me Tyrone. You're about to buy my home and property and I think formalities aren't necessary."

"Of course, Tyrone. How are you today?"

"Oh, getting along. I made some coffee, would you like some?"

"Sure, that sounds great. I take it black," James said nervously. He felt as if he was intruding.

"Come into the living room and we can talk in there," Tyrone offered.

"I appreciate you letting me come here today to see your home. I wanted to check it out more closely and see what needs repairing and redoing," James commented.

"I'm afraid quite a bit actually. I haven't had the strength or the money to redo very much around here. It's getting to be too much to handle. That's why I'm selling, but I have to admit that it's breaking my heart a little bit. I had a good life here, and this house and land has been in my family for many years. I don't expect you to understand that since you're in the business of buying up land and developing it for profit," Tyrone said bluntly.

"I do understand, Tyrone. I'm not heartless. You're right though, I do this to make money, but also do it to give people up-to-date living conditions, and upscale shopping and entertainment. I think they deserve this. The setting for all of this is phenomenal and I think it will work. Have you been having problems with the people of this community since you've been dealing with me?" James asked.

"Are you kidding? I'm lucky they even say two words to me lately. That's been hard. But when the sale is final, I plan to move in with my daughter in Seattle and I won't have to hear the anger from these people. You will though, are you prepared for that?" Tyrone asked James.

"I'm used to it. Being in this business has also been hard for me where people are concerned. No one likes land developers. They treat us like alien invaders," James lamented.

"Well, let's take a tour of the house so you can see what you're in for," Tyrone teased.

James was having a great time hearing the history of this house as Tyrone showed him every room. There were some plumbing problems as well as electrical. These would have to be taken care of before people would be allowed to come through and see the home. Ackerman Associates planned on making this house a place that people could walk through and pay an entrance fee. The grounds would be landscaped beautifully with the local flowers and trees and people would enjoy sitting on the benches and hearing docents telling them the history of the place.

They finished the tour in the kitchen. It was a large room and had modern appliances added in. There was also an eating area with bench type seats. Many cabinets were hanging on the walls, and the floor had linoleum on it. James was thinking to himself what he would do to slightly update the interior of the house. He didn't say anything because he didn't want to hurt Tyrone's feelings with his ideas. James loved the house and wouldn't mind living in it himself. His wife would love this place. He was startled out of his thoughts by Tyrone's comments.

"So, James, how do you like this house? It has a lot of room and a lot of history. You've probably been redecorating it in your mind, right?" Tyrone said, hitting the nail on the head.

"Maybe a little. It's a lovely house, Tyrone. We won't change that much. We'll honor your heritage of this place. Thank you for your hospitality and the coffee. I'll talk to you soon. I'll set up a meeting where you can come to Seattle to our offices so we can show you the plans in their entirety so you can get a better idea of what we plan to do," James offered.

"I'd appreciate that. Have a safe ride back to Seattle."

# CHAPTER FIVE

URING THE SUMMER MONTHS IN Blissville the weather was unpredictable. Up north it could be sunny, rainy, cold, hot, or just pleasant with no extremes. It was Saturday and the Warren household was busy rising to meet the day. Robert and Elise were going to work in the hardware store most of the day. Scotty woke up with a definite plan in his mind.

He washed up and walked down the hall to Meg's room. He knocked on her door.

"Who is it?" Meg sleepily mumbled.

"It's Scotty. Can I come in?"

"Yeah."

"Did I wake you up?"

"No. That's all right. What's up?"

"I really want to go to that place we went to last week where I found the bubbling spring."

"I've been thinking about it too. I'd like to explore it a little more. I'll call Billy and see if he wants to join us."

"Yay!!"

"Shhh. I don't want mom and dad to find out about it yet. Keep quiet."

"Sorry. I forgot. What's the big secret anyway?"

"I don't know. I just have a feeling that there's more to this than it seems. Go on, get out of here so I can get dressed."

Scotty ran downstairs and poured himself a bowl of cereal.

"Good morning young man. What's on your agenda today?" Elise asked Scotty.

"Not much. I think Meg and Billy and I are going hiking around the river. What are you doing today?"

"Working at the store. Your father's already there and I'll go in a little later this morning. Be careful hiking around that river. It's easy to get lost around there. I'm glad Meg and Billy will be with you."

"You never let me go there by myself anyway, Mom. I always go with Meg and Billy."

"You're right about that. One thing you do have when you go anywhere, is a good sense of direction. I remember when we all went to Seattle and we were trying to find a particular street that had a park on it and just couldn't find it. You popped up with an idea about going a couple blocks down the road and turning left and there lo and behold we found it. That was pretty good on your part. You have built in radar!"

"Good morning Mom," Meg said, walking slowly into the kitchen yawning.

"Hello sleepy head. What time did you go to sleep last night?" Elise asked.

"I got interested in a book I'm reading and didn't fall asleep until about 2 am."

"Serves you right. Well, have fun today hiking around the river. It's a beautiful day."

"I'm going to call Billy and see if he's free."

Meg went to her room and dialed Billy from her cell phone.

"Hey, good morning. How's it going?" Billy asked.

"Good. Scotty and I want to go to the place we went to last week with the spring. Are you free to join us? I hope so, because I don't think I can find it again."

"Sure. My parents are busy today. Mom has a big dinner she has to cook for the McCreedys, and Dad is working overtime at the lumber company. What time are you picking me up?"

"Is half an hour okay? I hope we can find this place."

"If anyone can find it, it's Scotty."

"True. He's the one who suggested we go today. I don't know. I have a strange feeling about that place."

"You just have a big imagination, that's all," Billy teased.

"See you in a bit. Oh, I'll pick up some sandwiches at the deli for us before I come to your house," Meg offered.

An hour passed, and Meg drove to the river with Billy and Scotty. She was feeling a little apprehensive. Elkwa River was particularly beautiful today. The water was still and clear and reflected the mountains surrounding it. At the lodge, a few people were taking boats out and rowing a distance away from the dock. Some people were jumping into the river around the dock and yelping because the water was so cold. Children were laughing and various people were sitting on the lounge chairs reading their books.

Meg parked the car at the river and they all got out. Meg and Billy didn't know which trail to take and Scotty said, "This way guys. Follow me."

Meg and Billy just looked at each other and rolled their eyes.

After a while the three of them reached a familiar place where they had sat down last time they were there. Meg recognized the rock she sat on.

"Aha, I remember it now. Scotty, do not run off like you did before. You can lead us to the spot with the water, but do it slowly with us walking behind you. Okay?" Meg asked with authority.

"Yes sergeant!" Scotty retorted with a salute. The three of them laughed and started on their way with lunch in hand.

"The birds are particularly noisy today aren't they?" Meg noticed.

"Yeah, they are. We're probably disturbing them," Billy answered.

"I think we're almost there guys. Look, I remember that big tree over there," Scotty said happily.

They walked several yards further to the big cedar tree that Scotty remembered when they were there last. Each of them found a rock to sit on to eat their lunch. It was a beautiful spot.

"I love this place. It's so peaceful," Billy reflected.

"It sure is. Scotty, we owe it to you. You're the one who found this place. I love all the cedar trees circling this spot," Meg said quietly.

They started to eat their lunch when Billy said, "Hey guys, I don't hear any birds here now. I wonder why they stopped chirping. Also where's the bubbling water we found before?"

"You're right about that, Billy," Meg agreed.

Just then, Scotty jumped up from the rock he was sitting on and said, "Whoa, did you guys see that?"

"See what?" Meg asked.

"I didn't see anything," Billy added.

"Out of the corner of my eye I saw something move fast over there," Scotty said apprehensively, pointing at the massive cedar tree to the right of where he was sitting.

"I think your imagination is running wild, Scotty," Meg commented.

"No. Honest, I feel weird in here. It's too quiet or something. Let's leave. I'm a little scared," Scotty admitted.

"Really Scotty, there's nothing to be scared of. We'll protect you. There are no animals here, and there's no one else here with us. Finish your lunch and we'll leave," Meg reassured him.

Scotty reluctantly finished his lunch not saying much of anything the remaining time they were there.

As they were driving back home, all three of them were wondering why they didn't see the water like before, and also why the birds stopped chirping in that area. Also, Scotty didn't let them forget that he saw something or someone out of the corner of his eye. He wasn't imagining it. It left him feeling uneasy.

# CHAPTER SIX

TYRONE BLAKE WAS PREPARING TO go to Seattle to have a meeting with James Ackerman, the land developer, to finalize the plans for Ackerman Associates to buy his land and the house he was living in. It took effort for Tyrone to take this trip, as he was getting old and was sick. Finalizing this deal and moving out of the house couldn't come fast enough for him.

Tyrone's trip on the plane was very pleasant. The flight attendants were accommodating, and he enjoyed the attention and service. When he arrived in Seattle, he took a cab to Ackerman's office.

"Hello Mr. Blake, please come in and sit down," Charise said with a smile on her face.

Charise McClelland had worked for Ackerman Associates for 10 years. She was James Ackerman's personal assistant and basically ran the office.

"James will be with you in a moment. He's finishing another meeting he had this afternoon. Would you like a cup of coffee?" Charise offered.

"I'd love some, thank you."

After ten minutes of small talk, Charise led Tyrone into James' office.

"Good afternoon Tyrone. I hope I didn't keep you waiting long," James said extending his hand.

"No not at all. Your secretary was kind and offered me coffee."

"Good. Have a seat please."

"When do you think you will be breaking ground on my property? I don't mean to rush you or anything, but I'm anxious to get out of there. My daughter's been nagging me about moving in with her and her husband. Everybody's anxious about the whole thing."

"Come let me show you what we have planned for your property. I think you will be pleased."

James took Tyrone into a big room with a huge table in the middle of it, with a scale model of the whole condominium complex, shopping mall, and the plans for refurbishing the home to be used as an historical landmark with tours for people to go inside.

"I can't believe this is happening. It's beautiful and very complex. You've taken on quite a bit of work here," Tyrone said in amazement.

"That's what we do, Tyrone. I want to make this an important part of Blissville, and a place where people can enjoy themselves and make new friends and also to have a lot of shopping opportunities."

"I hope you don't run into any trouble while doing this. The people there are very angry about me selling my property to you."

"I know they are. But when they see what we're offering to them, they'll change their minds."

"Tyrone, I'd like to take you to dinner this evening. Are you leaving in the morning?"

"Yes, I am. I'd be happy to have dinner with you."

# CHAPTER SEVEN

THE TOWN AND ALL THE citizens were getting ready for a huge barbecue potluck in Blake Park, which was named after Tyrone's family as far back as anyone could remember. There was an array of food from everyone. Elise especially loved the barbecue so she could make all her favorite and famous foods. Tyrone was invited, of course, but he wasn't sure he should be there because people weren't very happy with him of late. In the past, he always brought homemade pork sausage made from his pigs. His chickens and pigs had dwindled down because of the care they took. He was in the process of selling what he had left. However, he did make a batch of pork sausage and was planning on bringing some to the barbecue and then leaving quickly so as not to make people angry.

"Wow, it's hot today. I'll have to make sure to wear a hat so as not to get burned," Elise commented.

"I know. I'll bring one too. It should be fun with all the food and games. Dunking for apples is my game. Hey Scotty, are you going to go apple dunking?" Meg asked.

"Nah. You'll win that for sure. I like the ball games. I'm a good batter and I like to run the bases," Scotty said.

"I'd better go on ahead and help with the structure of the stage so the band can play for the dancing. I hope I can have the first dance with you my dear," Robert said romantically to Elise, while taking her in his arms and dancing around the kitchen floor.

The kids laughed and started dancing with each other. Scotty was stepping all over Meg's feet and laughing hysterically. There were mounds of salad, homemade pies, and lots of sandwiches on the Warren's table.

Robert left early to start help building the stage. The barbecue started around 1 pm and usually went on into the night. There were craft booths covering a wide area. Also, there were many tables and chairs and picnic benches scattered all around the park. Meg volunteered to help her friend, Marcy, with her booth. Marcy made beaded jewelry. It was a very popular booth each year. The food was put on tables in the center of where the tables and chairs were. People could go up and serve themselves when they wanted to eat. There were many shade trees in the park. Cedar, Douglas Fir, and some beautiful rhododendrons covered the gorgeous landscape.

Everyone was having a great time. Scotty batted two home runs in the baseball game that was set up, and music was playing from the band, and people were enjoying the wonderful food. A happy time was had by all in Blissville.

At 3 o'clock Tyrone came to the park with a big platter of homemade sausages. He was greeted by several of the townspeople who gladly took the platter from him and placed it in a special place on the food table. They loved his sausage. He started to leave when Tom and Lottie Chapman asked him to stay.

"Tyrone, stay and enjoy the festivities with us. There's plenty of food and some nice music from the band. Come sit down and I'll fix you a plate," Lottie offered with a smile on her face.

Tyrone couldn't say no to such kindness and agreed to stay for a while. He was a little hungry even though his pain medication curbed his appetite. He was a little embarrassed because of the sale of his land, but he had to do it. No one else offered to buy his property except the land developer.

"This is mighty good potato salad Lottie. Did you make it?" Tyrone asked.

"No, Elise made it. She's a wonderful cook, but you know that already," Lottie smiled.

"You're a good cook too with your catering and all. How's that business doing by the way?" Tyrone asked.

"Very well, Tyrone. Thanks for asking. I had a big party last weekend for 50 people and everyone loved the food. There wasn't much left after everyone left," Lottie said proudly.

After about an hour, Tyrone left the barbecue. He enjoyed the little time he spent there. Elise and Robert came up to him also and conversed for a while before he left. He could see people talking in a huddle and looking over at him. He knew they were talking about him. He couldn't take it any longer.

Billy and Meg were dancing to the band's music later in the day. Things were winding down and everyone was filled with the sumptuous food and also happy joining in on the games and festivities. It was another successful barbecue for the town of Blissville.

# CHAPTER EIGHT

T HE SUN WAS SHINING AND there were a few scattered fleecy clouds. It was very still outside with a few chirping birds to add to the serene atmosphere surrounding Blissville and its outlying areas. Everyone in the Warren's household was sleeping late this Saturday morning. Robert even put a sign on the door of the hardware store on Friday that business was open at noon today. They all needed much rest after preparations for the annual barbecue last weekend. They never really caught up with the rest they needed until this weekend. Meg's cell rang and she answered it.

"Why are you calling at this hour, Billy? We're sleeping in this morning."

"I'm sorry. I didn't realize you guys were being lazy today," Billy teased.

"We worked hard last weekend and my folks haven't caught up yet."

"What's your excuse?"

"Ha, ha, very funny. I took advantage of the quiet around here. That is, until the phone rang!"

"How about going to our favorite spot by the river? It's a gorgeous day," Billy suggested."

"Sure. No need to ask Scotty. I know he'll want to go."

"See you around 10. Is that okay?" Billy asked.

"Sounds good. See you then."

Elise slowly walked into the kitchen, yawning.

"Hi Mom. The three of us are going to the river today. It's a beautiful day out there. If you peek through the curtain you can see it's sunny and clear," Meg teased.

"Okay. Be careful guys."

Elise poured a cup of coffee and went back to her room. She was enjoying this rare time of quiet and peace and was taking every advantage of it. Robert was still asleep.

Meg, Scotty, and Billy arrived at the river. They couldn't believe how beautiful the weather was. They picked up some sandwiches and sodas from the deli in town. They started walking the half mile to the spot where they saw the bubbling spring. Scotty was being very quiet and Meg and Billy asked him why.

"What's going on Scotty?" Meg asked.

"Yeah, you seem so quiet. You're usually excited about coming here," Billy chimed in.

"It's nothing. I just...well, remember last time I saw something out of the corner of my eye? I felt stupid. I think you guys probably thought I was nuts!"

"Of course not, Scotty. It was a weird day and we all felt that we needed to leave. Don't worry about it. If you see anything again, we'll leave and won't talk about it," Meg reassured her brother.

"If I see anything, I want to know what it is. I won't be scared this time. You guys are with me and I'm protected, right?"

"Right, buddy," Billy said, patting Scotty on the back.

They each eventually found their rock to sit on and started to eat their lunch.

"Hey guys, the birds are quiet again like last time. What the heck is going on?" Billy asked a little puzzled.

"That's true. Strange," Meg agreed.

Scotty was staring at the place where the bubbling spring gurgled last time. Suddenly, water started coming up from it. A little bit at first, then a little more powerful a few seconds later.

"Hey, look at that!" Meg commented.

"It's so strange how it starts and stops. Maybe it knows when there's somebody around to see it," Billy said laughingly.

"Don't make fun of it, Billy. There's a reason for it. We just don't know what it is," Scotty said seriously.

"No need to get so serious Scotty," Meg retorted.

Scotty stared at the spring and Meg and Billy were starting to get worried about him. They never saw him this serious about anything. He was always playful and light hearted about things. Now they were getting a little nervous.

"I don't know guys. I feel weird and anxious and I don't know why," Scotty shared.

"Do you want to go home, Scotty?" Meg asked.

"No. I think we need to stay for some reason. Don't ask me why."

Meg and Billy looked at each other puzzled. They didn't know what to think or what to do at this point. They followed Scotty's lead for reasons they didn't understand.

All of a sudden the spring was bubbling at a very high volume and was producing more water than they ever saw.

As they were looking at it in shock, a mist began to appear before them on the other side of the spring from where they were sitting. Their mouths were agape at the apparition they were seeing develop before their eyes.

"Yeah!!! I think that's what I saw last time we were here," Scotty said excitedly.

All three of them stood up and were feeling apprehensive, excited, and curious about what they were seeing. The apparition became clearer and what they saw before them was unbelievable and exciting at the same time.

"It's an Indian! A real Indian!" Scotty shouted.

"You're absolutely right, Scotty," Meg and Billy said at the same time.

"Who are you?" Scotty asked with enthusiasm and awe.

The apparition looked at the three of them standing by the spring, and came forward a few steps. When he came forward, the three of them stepped back a few steps. They were still a little fearful of what they were seeing. The Indian had one white feather attached to the back of the band that was surrounding his forehead. He had on pale leather pants, moccasins, and a fringed leather top with strands of beads around his neck. His face was wrinkled with age and wisdom. He had gentle eyes that looked right through you.

"I am Chief White Feather. I come from the Elkwha tribe who lived and survived in this area. We ate salmon from the river, clams from the ocean, and berries and roots from the forests. We killed elk and bear. We only killed what we needed to survive. We respected the land and gave thanks for the bounties it gave us. You people are ravaging this land and you are making the spirits angry."

Meg, Billy, and Scotty stood there quietly and didn't know what to say. Their mouths were agape and they felt nervous. They felt as if the chief was accusing them of the ravaging. They loved this land and respected it. Scotty was the first to speak up.

"Were you here before, Chief? I saw something and we took off kind of scared," Scotty asked.

"Yes. Don't be afraid. I come here out of necessity and for your town and its people's safety. You must stop this building that is going to start shortly. This is sacred land. It must not be destroyed, because if it happens, your town will experience a giant flood. This spring you see is from Mother Earth. It is from an artesian well under this land and gurgles with anger when you're around to see it. You are the messengers for this problem and must tell those you love and the town and the man who owns this land to "stop." No building on this land."

With that, he disappeared slowly and the mist was gone. The three of them were cemented to the ground. They couldn't move. They had a lot to digest.

"What the heck was that?" Billy asked bewildered.

"An Indian chief," Meg answered.

"Yeah, it sure was. Wow!!! I have chills from that. Do you have chills?" Scotty asked the other two.

"More than chills. I'm freaked," Meg stated.

"You're not the only one," Billy agreed.

"Guys! We have an important job to do. Did you hear him? We're the messengers and have to warn everyone about old Tyrone selling his land to that builder...what's his name?" Scotty said excitedly.

"James Ackerman. This whole thing is the talk of the town. Everyone is so upset about it. I didn't know this was sacred land, did you guys know about it?" Meg asked.

"No. But wherever Indian tribes lived, which is pretty much everywhere, there's bound to be sacred land in all of those places. Our own houses could be on sacred land. Who knows?" Billy said.

"I doubt that Billy. We would have found out about it before now. We need to talk about this, but not here. Let's get together tomorrow and discuss what we're going to do. Do not tell our parents about it yet, because we don't know enough about it to discuss it with them," Meg stated.

"Yeah, you're right. That was so weird. I never believed in ghosts before, but now…..," Billy said bewildered.

"We can thank Scotty for this experience," Meg said.

"Hey, don't blame me for that Indian showing up. Actually, he was pretty cool. I loved his feather and his clothes. I feel that he's a nice man. He's just a little angry about this land."

"Let's get going. I think we've had enough for one day," Meg said a little agitated.

# CHAPTER NINE

MEG, SCOTTY, AND BILLY MET at Billy's house and discussed what they had witnessed at the spring the day before. They were still pretty well shaken up about it. Billy had a big tree house in the backyard that his father had built for him two years before. They met up there and went over the experience.

"Wow, that was something yesterday. I never thought I would see a ghost like that," Scotty said excitedly.

"I know, it was pretty cool," Billy agreed.

"I need to tell you guys something," Meg said nervously. "It happened right after Grandma Claire died. I was sleeping and suddenly I woke up with a start. Grandma's face was real close to mine and was very clear. I was wide awake after that. It was proof we don't really die. We just cross over to the other side."

"You never said anything about that, Meg. Why?" Scotty asked.

"What would you have thought if I did?"

"Well, that's true. I probably would have thought you lost it!!" Scotty teased.

"That's amazing, Meg. Have you had any other experiences like that?" Billy asked seriously.

"I just didn't want you guys to be frightened by what we saw yesterday. I think those who have gone before us come back when there is something important they need to say or do. With Grandma, I didn't know why she did that. Maybe it was to let me know that she was still around."

"Whatever the reason, I think it's so cool. We have an important job to do with this information Chief White Feather told us. I'm just afraid that people will think we're all nuts," Billy said solemnly.

"I don't care what people think. We saw him and we experienced it. That's it. Mr. Blake and that builder can't build on the land by the river. It's sacred. We need to stop them," Scotty stated.

"Please don't say anything yet. We need to think about this and plan our strategy carefully so as not to hurt anyone or anything. This is quite a responsibility put on us. I wonder why he chose us?" Meg pondered.

"Maybe he knew that we understood about spirits and everything. We didn't freak out too much when he came to us, did we?" Scotty asked.

"Probably the next time we won't be so frozen in our tracks," Billy remarked.

"Can you imagine what our parents are going to think when we tell them? They'll say we have an overactive imagination. We may have to bring them to our favorite spot next to the river and prove to them that there's something going on," Meg suggested.

"That's a great idea. That way, the more people getting involved the more they can help stop this mess," Billy agreed.

The three of them left the tree house and went their separate ways.

# CHAPTER TEN

ACKERMAN ASSOCIATES BROKE GROUND ON Tyrone Blake's property. They started halfway between the house and the edge of the property near the Elkwa River. They moved quickly, and were already starting to build. Tyrone had moved in with his daughter in Seattle and was settled there. His daughter took him to therapy for his colon cancer, which was getting worse. He was given drugs to help him with the pain and discomfort. He was a brave man. Ackerman Associates had Tyrone's number in case there was a problem. Tyrone said that they could contact him in case anything came up that needed his attention.

It was noisy with the equipment being used to dig out the dirt on the property. The people of the town were complaining about the noise and the fact that beautiful property was being changed into a commercial business to make money. While the digging was going on, Meg, Scotty, and Billy decided that they wanted to explore the area that was being dug up. They waited until later when the workers were finished for the day.

"I hope nobody's around here while we're being nosy," Billy warned.

"Don't worry, we would hear some kind of noise if they were," Meg answered.

Scotty was busy exploring around in the dirt, and let out a yelp of discovery.

"Wow, look at this," Scotty said excitedly.

"An arrowhead!!! How cool is that?" Billy said.

"I wonder what else is on this land. Chief White Feather was right about this being sacred land. That arrowhead proves it," Meg said compassionately.

All three of them were busy poking around in the dirt. They each gathered twigs from nearby to help with the digging. They were silent with concentration and excitement, wondering what they were going to come up with.

Meg noticed a mound close by and her gut feeling was telling her to explore it. As she was digging into it, in the clumps of dirt were imbedded Indian beads. She couldn't believe what she was seeing.

"Oh my!! Look at this, guys," Meg said with excitement and concern.

"What are those beads for?" Scotty asked.

"From what I've read, when any member of the tribe dies, they bury them with their possessions. They made necklaces and other pieces of jewelry to wear. This is a burial ground guys. It's sacred. This is not good," Meg said worriedly.

"Let's take a few clumps of dirt and the arrowhead back with us. This will be a good way to bring this whole problem up with our parents. They're more apt to believe us with this evidence," Billy suggested.

"Great idea. Actually, I heard mom talking about asking your parents over tomorrow night, Billy, and she sort of hinted that she would like for the three of us to go to a movie or something. I guess it's parent's night. That'll work out though, because that way we can work out a strategy on how to tell them without sneaking around," Meg said.

"We'll have dinner at the Hamburger Palace, and then go see a movie," Billy suggested.

"Sounds like a plan. Here, I brought some ziplock bags in case we found something. It looks like we did!" Meg said enthusiastically.

"Hey, I found another arrowhead," Scotty said, elated with his find.

As they were preparing to leave, Billy discovered something in the distance from the mound. It was a large rock, and the center of it was smoothed out and had a deep impression. He was trying to figure out what it was used for.

"Look at this, guys. What do you think this was used for," Billy asked.

"That's so exciting. It was used for grinding seeds, and probably corn to make meal out of it. They used a tool to grind with. We can't take that with us because it's too heavy. When we bring our parents back here to show them what we've discovered they'll see it. Let's get going guys, and we'll hide these things until we tell them what's going on," Meg suggested.

The three of them quietly walked to the car and were deep in thought of what they discovered. They were also worried about the consequences of this find. They were hoping to see Chief White Feather soon to tell him about their findings. They wanted to know what to do with it.

# CHAPTER ELEVEN

"**C**OME IN, COME IN. IT's so good to see you. How are you guys?" Elise said to the Chapmans, Lottie and Tom.

"Wonderful, how are you?" Lottie asked.

"Busy as ever at the store. It never ends. We practically live there!" Robert commented.

"Owning one's own business is certainly a full time commitment," Tom added.

"Come sit down and enjoy the appetizers I made for us," Elise said. "What would you two like to drink? We have wine, sodas, or sparkling apple juice," Elise suggested.

"Wine sounds good," Tom stated.

"Then wine it is. What about you Lottie? What would you like?" Elise asked.

"Actually, the sparkling apple juice sounds very good," Lottie answered.

They all enjoyed the appetizers and drinks and were starting out with small talk. As the conversation progressed though, they all started talking about the peculiar behavior of their kids lately.

"Have you noticed Billy acting a little secretive lately? The reason I ask is that Meg and Scotty certainly have. All three of them seem to be involved in something that has sparked their interest and they always go to the river. What do you think?" Elise asked the Chapmans.

"Funny you should ask," Tom stated.

"Yeah, Elise and I are somewhat concerned about it. When we ask where they're going they give us short answers and change the subject," Robert added.

"As a matter of fact, just yesterday I was curious where they'd been and when I asked Billy what kind of day the three of them had he said fine!" Tom said bewildered.

"That's exactly what I'm talking about," Elise said.

"Maybe we're reading too much into this. After all, summer is for exploring and everything. Maybe they're curious about the building going on with Tyrone's property. They spend a lot of time over there. The property is near the river, and maybe that's why they're going there so often. Let's just ask them when they come home," Robert suggested.

"Okay. I won't say anything more about it. How's your personal chef business doing Lottie?" Elise asked.

"Great. I've gotten two more families. The mother has to work now and doesn't have time to cook every night. I go over there three times a week and cook for them. I prepare enough so that there are leftovers for them to eat when I'm not there. I'm lucky to have families who enjoy it when I experiment with different recipes and surprise them with a menu I've come up with," Lottie related.

"That's wonderful. Well, I've sampled many of your meals and they're so delicious and innovative. You're great with spices and know how to use them in the different dishes you prepare," Elise said, complimenting Lottie on her talents in the kitchen.

"Speaking of food, I better check on the leg of lamb I've prepared for us. I like it a little pink inside and not too overdone, how about you guys?" Elise asked.

"Absolutely. It gets like leather if too overcooked. Can I help you with anything?" Lottie offered.

"Maybe you could toss the salad if you wouldn't mind," Elise suggested.

"I don't mind at all. I love working in the kitchen," Lottie said.

As Lottie and Elise were busy in the kitchen, Robert and Tom were talking in the living room. The subject of the kids and the building site came up again.

"So what do you really think about all that building going on at Tyrone's old place?" Tom asked.

"I don't like it one bit. It's a beautiful property and should have been sold to a family who was looking for a place to either grow vegetables, or who loved horses and had a ranch, or anyone else besides a builder who wants to make it a commercial property. It's ridiculous and pathetic to do this," Robert answered.

"We should ask the kids what their opinion is about it. What do you think?" Tom asked.

"Let's do it. When they get home we'll ask them. They spend enough time around the river area to have thoughts on the subject," Robert added.

"Dinner's ready! Bring your appetites guys," Elise shouted.

"I'm ready to eat, how about you?" Robert asked Tom.

"Show me the grub!!!" Tom answered.

# Chapter Twelve

As the Warrens and the Chapmans were finishing their dessert in the living room, the kids came home after seeing a movie.

"How was the movie, guys?" Tom Chapman asked.

"Great. How was dinner?" Meg answered back.

"As you can see we look quite content. Don't you agree?" Elise commented.

"We need to talk to you guys about your visits to the river. We can sense that you all are keeping something from us and we need to know what it is. Am I correct in assuming this is true?" Robert asked.

"Uh, yeah, I guess so," Billy stammered.

"It's okay Billy, our parents need to know what's happening. It's for everybody's safety," Meg warned.

"What are you talking about, Meg?" Robert asked worriedly.

"It's a long story, Dad, but if you guys have the time we'll tell you," Meg said.

"We're all ears!" Lottie interjected.

"Yes, we are," Elise added.

"Well, it started weeks ago," Meg started to say.

"The three of us were having a picnic by the river near Tyrone Blake's property and enjoying the scenery and quiet. Then we walked into the woods further and heard running water," Billy was saying with excitement.

"Yeah, then I ran ahead and there it was," Scotty said enthusiastically.

"There was what?" Robert asked.

The three kids told the whole story to their parents, and they were all trying to talk at once and interrupting each other with all of their excitement. The parents were sitting there with their mouths open and with a look of utter amazement on their faces.

"You mean to tell me that you actually saw this Indian chief?" Tom asked with a little disbelief in his voice.

"Yes Dad. Really. We aren't making this up," Billy said, trying to convince the parents about all of this.

"I think we should all go to this spot they're talking about. Don't you agree?" Elise asked.

"That would be great Mom. That way, you won't think we're making this up," Meg commented.

"Meg, it isn't that we don't believe you guys. It's...well, you have to admit it's a wild story. However, if this is true it could pose danger for this town. I know that Indian legend and beliefs are very strong. We need to honor and respect them," Elise said seriously.

"Since when do you know so much about Indian legend? I didn't know you felt so strongly about it," Robert said questionably.

"My mother was a very strong believer in the supernatural and spirits. She came to me after her death and it scared me, but it also instilled in me the fact that we don't die when we leave this earth," Elise continued.

"Mom, Grandma Claire came to me also after she died. I didn't know that happened to you too. Why didn't you tell me?" Meg asked with tears in her eyes.

"I didn't want to scare you sweetheart. I didn't know how much you believed what Grandma told you in the past."

"I can't believe all of this. It's creepy but interesting all at the same time," Tom stated.

"I certainly believe this could happen. I've had a few interesting experiences in my lifetime too," Lottie interjected.

"Such as?" Tom asked.

"I don't want to get into it now. Later. We have more important things to decipher first. Okay, how about tomorrow after breakfast we pack a lunch and have a picnic like the kids did and see we what we come up with," Lottie suggested.

"Sounds good to me. I'll close up shop for part of the day. I'll put my "Gone Fishing" sign up on the door," Robert teased.

"We have something to show you guys. Meg, do you have the arrowheads and beads we found," Scotty asked.

"Yes, I'll go get them," Meg said as she ran into her bedroom.

"Arrowheads and beads? Where did you find them, Scotty?" Elise asked concerned.

"They were lying there on the edge of Blake's property. I guess they became easier to find with all of their digging and bulldozing," Scotty informed them.

"Here they are. Aren't they beautiful?" Meg said as she handed them to her mom.

Elise very carefully handled the arrowheads and the clump of dirt which held the beads. There was silence in the living room as they all looked at these items with awe. The kids looked at each other with smiles on their faces and were so pleased that their parents weren't mad but very intrigued with it all. They also knew that their parents wouldn't put up with any danger happening to their town.

"I sure hope Chief White Feather shows up tomorrow. It would be so cool," Scotty said with enthusiasm.

"Don't worry. I think he will be there. He wanted us to spread the news of impending danger, and we did. I think our parents are going to be very impressed," Meg said.

"I'm really getting excited about this. Life is certainly not dull around here," Billy added.

"Okay guys. This is impressive indeed. There are hundreds of beads imbedded in this clump of dirt. They belonged to someone in a tribal family. They could be considered sacred. We really need to go there and see what's happening and find out what to do about it," Elise said pointedly.

"Absolutely. I think we should go home guys and sleep on this. We need to be fresh and have our wits about us tomorrow as we embark on this adventure," Lottie stated.

"Okay. Thank you for coming over for dinner you two. Don't ever say that we don't provide entertainment for our guests," Elise teased.

"That's an understatement! I'm actually looking forward to this," Lottie said.

Both Robert and Tom rolled their eyes and played along with the kids and their wives. They weren't sure whether to believe all of this or not. They were the skeptics. They made jokes about it and went along with everyone else but felt in their gut that it was all a hoax.

# CHAPTER THIRTEEN

THE KIDS FROM BOTH FAMILIES were up and ready early the next morning. They fixed breakfast for their parents and started packing their lunches for the picnic at the river.

"Mom and Dad, get up! We have important business to take care of," Meg yelled.

"You tell them! I'm kind of nervous about this, Meg. How about you?" Scotty asked.

"No need to be nervous, Scotty. We've been there several times, and now we're just inviting our parents to come and see for themselves. What could go wrong? Worst case scenario, the Chief won't show up. Then we would look like liars! But I don't think that will happen. The Chief is pretty serious about this happening. He'll be there," Meg reassured Scotty.

"Good morning, you two. Is breakfast ready?" Robert asked with a smile on his face. He was having fun with all of this.

"Have a seat Dad. Enjoy. You're taking this very lightly aren't you?" Meg asked with sarcasm in her voice.

"What? I'm going to the river aren't I," Robert said innocently.

"Good morning guys. Thanks for making breakfast. Did you pack a lunch?" Elise asked yawning.

"Yes, we're in the process of packing one. I wonder if Billy and his parents are up yet. I think I'll go and call," Meg stated.

Billy picked up the phone as it rang.

"Yeah, we're getting there. Mom was up early making breakfast and packing our lunch. Dad is taking his time. I think he thinks this is a game," Billy observed.

"I think the same thing about my dad. Well, I can't wait to see the expressions on their faces when Chief White Feather shows up. Can you imagine?" Meg asked.

"I'll bring my camera. See you in half an hour," Billy said.

Both families piled in their cars and drove to the Elkwa River. It was a beautiful sunny day and the birds were chirping away among the trees.

"This is really close to Blake's property isn't it? I didn't realize how close," Tom observed.

"I knew it was close but I agree, I didn't realize the proximity of the river to his acreage," Robert answered.

Everyone gathered their backpacks and put their lunches into them. They each had their bottle of water, sunglasses, and hats. They started their trek into the woods. Scotty was leading them to their destination. His sense of direction was right on target.

"Scotty, don't run off so fast. Take it easy," Elise was warning him.

"Don't worry Mom. He knows the way. Your son has a great sense of direction. Billy and I found that out when we were exploring this area on our own," Meg reassured her.

Tom and Robert were lagging behind talking about hunting, canoeing, and everything else besides what they were about to find out.

"Come on Dad. Act like you're interested," Billy said with impatience in his voice.

"We're coming, we're coming. Don't nag," Tom yelled.

As they approached the spot where the kids saw the apparition of Chief White Feather, it became very silent. No birds were chirping, and the sound of the river was fading as they walked further into the woods. Everyone was silent. It was as if they were waiting for something to happen.

Billy turned around to the dads and said "Boo!" He said it loud enough that the two men startled and looked embarrassed in doing it.

"Very cute, Billy. You think you're so smart!" Tom snapped.

"Here's the spot, guys. Everyone pick out a rock to sit on and let's start eating lunch," Scotty ordered.

"Okay boss! Notice how quiet everything is. Just like before," Billy observed.

"Yeah, I noticed. Hey guys, the spring isn't bubbling like before. Maybe today is different," Meg said with disappointment.

"You mean the spring comes and goes as it pleases?" Tom asked.

"Sort of. It kind of depends on whether Chief White Feather is near or not. I know it sounds crazy, but that's the way it works. We just have to be patient," Billy stated.

"These are good sandwiches you guys. You put together a good lunch in such a short time," Elise complimented.

"Thanks Mom," Meg answered.

"How's your lunch you two," Lottie asked her husband and son.

"Good," Tom answered while looking around as if something or someone was about to jump out and scare everyone.

"Relax. There's nothing to worry about. Let's just eat and talk and we'll see what happens," Meg suggested.

Meg put everyone at ease and they were eating, talking, joking around, and remembering old times coming to the river. As they were talking, Scotty looked to his right and noticed a little water bubbling up from the spring. He watched in silence while everyone else was preoccupied with their conversations. Meg looked over at Scotty and noticed his reaction and then looked at the spring which was bubbling a little faster.

"Uh, guys, the spring is making its presence known as we speak. Look over there," Meg said to the parents.

"Oh my God! There it is. It's gaining momentum as it's bubbling up," Lottie said with surprise in her voice.

Everyone got up and walked over to the spring which was now gurgling up a good amount of water. They were all exclaiming and were very excited about this.

"Let's just sit down and relax and wait to see what's going to happen next," Billy suggested.

"What do you expect is going to happen, Billy?" Tom asked with skepticism.

"Just wait and see Dad," Billy said.

"There, look, there's a white cloud sort of coming into view," Scotty said with excitement in his voice. He could hardly contain himself.

"Oh my! Scotty's right, Elise. I see it. It's getting stronger. I'm overwhelmed," Lottie said with a little fear.

"This reminds me of when my mother showed herself to me," Elise remembered.

The two men were standing there with their eyes wide open, mouths slightly agape, and their hearts pounding out of their chests. The kids looked over at them and smiled. They were waiting for this moment when their fathers would finally believe them.

"I see that you brought your parents today, children. That's good," Chief White Feather said. His voice always sounded like he was talking in an echo chamber.

"We told our parents all about what you said, Chief White Feather. They wanted to come to see for themselves," Meg said.

"Good. What do you have in your hands, child?" Chief White Feather asked.

"We found these beads and arrowheads in the dirt where the construction is going on. We're taking very good care of them," Meg said and she showed him what they found.

"Those belonged to my people. They lived on this ground. Those people must stop building and destroying the land. There are bodies of my family buried in that ground," Chief White Feather said with passion.

"We'll do all we can, Chief, we promise," Tom found himself saying without fear.

Lottie looked at him and smiled. Now he believed.

"Yes, we'll do what we can. We'll go talk to the builder ourselves and try and convince him to stop. We'll show him the arrowheads and beads and maybe he'll back down. Or at least change his mind about what to do with this land. Crops should grow on this land, enough to feed a lot of people. He could become a commercial grower. There're plenty of things to do here without destroying this sacred land. They could fix up the mansion and people would come and see it. They could eat and stay overnight in town instead of the hotel the builder wants to build," Robert said.

The whole family looked at Robert, surprised with the compassionate things he was saying. Elise was so proud that she went over to him and hugged him.

"That man will not listen. The Tribal Canoe Journey celebration will be happening next weekend. On that day, there will be a great flood happening if things don't stop now. This is a warning to you people! For more than ten thousand years our ancestors cared for the rivers, the forests, and meadows. In return, nature provided for us. We used cedar to build longhouses and canoes. We used bark to make clothing and to weave baskets. The rivers were full of salmon and the oceans were filled with clams, oysters and other fish. We ate berries and elk from the forests. Our tribes still care for this land today. We ask that you remember and care the same way," Chief White Feather informed them.

Chief White Feather's image started fading away. The bubbling spring subsided also. Both families were standing there in complete awe and silence. They all picked up their backpacks and silently started walking back to their cars. No one said a word. There was a silent understanding between them, and they had a lot to think about. Scotty was dying to say something and he did.

"Wasn't that cool? Now do you believe us?" Scotty asked.

After the silence was broken, everyone started talking at the same time.

# CHAPTER FOURTEEN

THE BUILDERS WERE BUSY WITH construction for the new mall. The Chapmans and the Warrens drove over to the site and asked the foreman if James Ackerman was present for them to talk to. Lucky for them he happened to be there that day.

"Hello Mr. Ackerman. I'm Elise Warren and this is my family. Also, our friends, the Chapmans are here with us. We need to talk to you about your construction of the mall."

"I have a makeshift office over here. Please join me for some coffee."

James Ackerman showed them to the tent he had set up with a desk, tables, chairs, a file cabinet, and a coffee maker. Outside were several portable bathrooms for crew and guests if needed.

"Please excuse the primitive facilities here, but as you can see we're working hard to bring this new center to everyone in the town of Blissville."

"That's why we're here, Mr. Ackerman," Elise said.

The rest of the two families sat quietly while Elise sort of took over the conversation to start with.

"Please call me James. Now what can I help you with?" Ackerman asked.

"This is going to sound a little crazy to you, but we completely believe what we are about to say to you. Please listen and take this information to heart. We're very concerned," Elise said with worry in her voice.

"I'm listening. I'll help as much as I can," Ackerman said politely.

"Meg, could you explain what has been happening lately by the river? The three of you kids know more than we do," Elise asked.

The three of them, Meg, Scotty, and Billy, stood up and cleared their throats and started talking. James was amused with what was happening and how serious everyone was. He let them speak and had a half smile on his face as he listened.

"Well, several weeks ago Scotty, Billy, and I were having a picnic by the river. We walked in pretty far and were enjoying the sound of the birds and scenery as we always do, when Scotty went up ahead of us and found something. We followed him and where we stopped, the birds weren't chirping anymore, and it was very silent except for the bubbling spring," Meg explained.

"The bubbling spring?" James asked.

"Yes. It doesn't always bubble, only when "he" appears," Scotty interjected.

"Excuse me. When who appears?" Ackerman asked, more and more amused.

"Scotty, let me tell the story, okay? You're jumping ahead of things," Meg suggested.

"Okay. Sorry," Scotty said a little disappointed.

"Mr. Ackerman, the three of us have seen a vision of an Indian chief named White Feather, and he has warned us of impending danger if you continue the building on this sacred land," Meg blurted out.

"Actually, all of us have seen this apparition, James. Not just the kids," Elise chimed in.

"Let me get this straight. You all have seen a "ghost" of an Indian chief warning you that we need to stop building?" Ackerman said with sarcasm in his voice.

"I know, it sounds far-fetched. But believe me it's true. We've seen him. This is something we need to listen to and heed," Robert added.

"Just what is going to happen if we continue to build?" James asked skeptically.

"A great flood. That's what's going to happen. It's supposed to happen on the day of the canoe journey of the tribes in Port Bliss. You need to listen to him and to us," Meg warned.

"She's right Mr. Ackerman. I was scared when I first saw this Indian chief, but he was kind to us and explained what this land meant to his people. Please listen. Look, we found these arrowheads and Indian beads on the far end of this property. There's also a grinding rock there where they ground seeds and stuff," Billy said, as he handed these things to Ackerman.

Ackerman looked at the arrowheads and beads that were imbedded in the clump of dirt, and mused on them for a few minutes. He turned them over and over and looked deep in thought.

"This is very interesting. I thank you all for expressing your concern over this, but please forget about the dangers you believe are going to happen. I assure you everything will be just fine. When we find anything pertaining to the Indian culture, we won't destroy it; we'll keep them intact and make it part of the tour of the restored house and all," Ackerman tried to reassure them.

"You don't understand, Mr. Ackerman. This land is sacred. You're destroying it. This is for real, not a fantasy we've made up," Lottie finally stated.

Through the whole conversation, Tom never said a word. He was still baffled by it all, and didn't know what to say, so he just listened.

"Thank you all for coming. Please don't be worried about this. We're very careful about what we're doing here. Next week we're starting to renovate the house. It will be beautiful and will make you proud of this town when we're finished with it all," Ackerman promised.

The two families looked disappointed at Ackerman, and his refusing to believe them about Chief White Feather and the warning. They left in a huff and drove back to the Warren's house.

"The flood is supposed to be happening when the canoe journey comes to the port. That leaves only six days from now. This is really scary," Scotty said.

"I think we need to go back to the spring and see if we can talk to Chief White Feather and tell him that we warned Ackerman. We did what we could. What else is there?" Elise asked.

"That sounds like a plan. We'll all go with you," Robert suggested.

"Absolutely. We'll pack another lunch and see what we come up with," Lottie added.

"This is crazy. Do you really believe all this stuff?" Tom finally asked.

"Why haven't you said anything, Tom?" Lottie asked. "You just stood there and didn't add to the conversation. Why?"

"I just think it's all too strange. Did we really see that Chief White Feather? I mean, really. I'm just finding it hard to completely believe it, that's all," Tom said.

Everyone stood there looking at Tom with disbelief. He was feeling very uncomfortable.

"Dad, it's okay. We believe it, so just go along with us and we'll all see what happens," Billy reassured him.

"Thanks son. I don't want to be the wet blanket, guys. Really. I'll go along with you and see what happens, like Billy said," Tom agreed.

They all hugged each other and said their goodbyes with smiles.

"Poor Tom. It's very hard to believe all of this. But I've learned from life that there is nothing that's impossible. Anything can happen," Robert said.

"Thank you Robert. That's absolutely true. We need to take this seriously. I'm not looking forward to next weekend. I hope we can settle this with Chief White Feather tomorrow," Elise said nervously.

They all went to bed without saying anything else about the construction and the flood.

# CHAPTER FIFTEEN

T HE WARRENS AND THE CHAPMANS drove to the river. They took out their lunches and drinks and started on their way to the spring. They walked along without saying much of anything. They were all a little nervous and concerned with the consequences of their visit with James Ackerman. Meg, Scotty, and Billy were leading the hike. Scotty ran ahead as he always did, and found the spring bubbling.

"Hey guys, the spring is bubbling. That means that the Chief is coming," Scotty said excitedly.

"I guess it does. I wonder if he knows what went on with Ackerman. Spirits know just about everything," Meg mused.

As they all walked up to the spring, they found their rock to sit on and started eating their sandwiches. The water was bubbling a little stronger than it normally did.

"Look at that water, guys. I've never seen it gushing so strongly," Meg noticed.

"I know. I wonder what that means," Billy asked.

"Maybe it means that we'll have a visitor soon," Elise added.

"This really makes me anxious. I'm not used to this type of thing," Tom said nervously.

"It's okay honey. Please don't be nervous. We're all here and nothing bad is going to happen," Lottie reassured him.

"Tom, let's take a little walk over there and check out those trees. It looks like a beautiful spot," Robert suggested.

"Sounds like a good idea. I could use a diversion," Tom said enthusiastically.

Tom and Robert took off and started talking about the river and fishing.

"That's nice of Robert to keep Tom busy so he won't be too anxious. He's feeling like a kid with all of this. The rest of us believe, but he's having a hard time with it," Lottie said.

"I'm so sorry about that. I admit I'm a little nervous also. After all, this stuff doesn't happen every day," Elise admitted.

"Hey guys, the birds stopped chirping. The water is also bubbling really hard now. I think Chief White Feather is coming," Scotty said anxiously.

As he said this, a faint white mist appeared before them. As they looked at it in awe, it grew denser and bigger. Finally, Chief White Feather made his presence known.

"Do you have information for me?" the Chief asked.

"Yes we do, Chief. Meg, tell him what happened with Ackerman yesterday," Scotty said with respect.

"We all went to see James Ackerman who is the builder at the property where they're constructing the new mall," Meg said nervously.

"And what did this Ackerman have to say?" Chief White Feather asked.

"We told him about the sacredness of the land, and we showed him the beads and the arrowheads and told him about the grinding rock. He looked at them and said not to worry about anything, that everything will be all right," Meg said.

"He doesn't care, Chief. We did what we could. What's going to happen?" Billy asked with concern in his voice.

"Thank you for trying to make this man listen. I knew he wouldn't, but he needs to know what he is doing. He will suffer the consequences. Please gather around and listen to what I have to say. I want to tell you about the canoe journey and what it means. I will also tell you what will happen to this sacred land," Chief White Feather said.

"Wait, Chief. Our dads are taking a walk. I'll go get them. I want them to hear this also," Billy said.

Billy found Tom and Robert and brought them back to hear what Chief White Feather had to say.

"Okay, we're all here now. What do you want to say to us, Chief?" Billy asked with anticipation.

"Our story is a timeless one and has great meaning for our people. We cherish this land and treat it with respect. Pollution, destruction, and the endangered population of the animals is all because of white man's hunger for money and wanting more and more without giving back. Tradition and respect of our people and of this Earth must never be forgotten by anyone who lives on this earth. What I'm about to tell you is a tradition for our people that has happened for many years and is a sight to behold."

As Chief White Feather was talking, he seemed to be floating off the ground about three feet, and had a very captive audience with the two families. They listened with respect and anticipation to what he was saying.

"This journey commemorates our canoe culture and brings together many tribes of this region of the world. There are about 80 ocean-going canoes that make a two-week journey from as far north as Alaska and as far south as Oregon. The canoes are painted in traditional Pacific Northwest colors. The journey ends when each canoe sails into the homeland of the host tribe. This year it is at Port Bliss where this journey ends. There will be singing and dancing and storytelling. Many people like you will be there to watch and enjoy this ceremony."

"It sounds wonderful, Chief White Feather. We've never seen this ceremony before. We always thought there would be too many people there and we wouldn't enjoy it as much," Meg commented.

"What does this ceremony of canoes have to do with what's going to happen if that builder continues his work?" Robert asked.

"What better time to show these builders what they are ruining and disrespecting? Mother Earth wants the people to feel, notice and develop a greater love for our planet than they do now. When the last canoe sails into the beach at Port Bliss, the power of the earth will make its presence known in this area right here. You see this bubbling spring? It won't be a calm bubbling spring any longer. Mother Earth's anger and tears will make you all aware of what you're doing to this planet and our sacred and beautiful land. This will all happen at the same time."

"What exactly is going to happen, Chief?" Elise asked, afraid of the answer.

"Yeah, what are we in for?" Scotty asked.

"I guess we all want to know what to expect and what to do about it for our protection," Tom added.

"I understand your concerns. I am compassionate for you people. You're not the ones building on our sacred land. Land where our forefathers are buried and our children. The north end of your town will be damaged from the power of the water gushing forth. Warn the people living there and tell them to leave their homes and businesses so they won't be killed. I'm sorry this has to happen but the forces of nature are strong and beyond anyone's control. Everything that happens is for good reason. We don't always see this right away, but afterwards the light shines and we understand."

"Wow!!! You mean this little spring right here is going to cause a flood?" Billy asked, bewildered.

"That's right, my son. There is powerful anger and strength below this land. Try all you can to warn this builder. This is not a joke. It's going to happen. It's time that man listens with his heart and not his pocketbook."

"Truer words have never been spoken Chief. We respect them and respect you and your people. I'm so sorry this is happening. This man won't listen to reason. He probably thinks we're crazy and overreacting. After the flood he'll think differently about it. I'm just glad we live in the south end of town. There aren't as many homes at the north end. That's where the public buildings are and a few businesses that aren't doing that well. Thank God it isn't in the heart of the town, because it would be more devastating," Lottie said with great concern.

"Mother Earth is not without compassion. No one will be killed because you will warn them as I have told you to do. This builder needs to see what damage he has caused and it should scare him to see this flood. People could have died because of this, but were spared. The most damage will be where he is building. The man who lived there treated that land with respect. He planted vegetables and would stand out there and admire the beauty of the trees and his surroundings. His house and the out buildings were the only things on the property. He survived on that land. This builder wants to make money and strip away everything of beauty in it. That won't happen. See what you can do to reason with him again. I will see you here next week and we will talk before the canoe journey."

The chief was fading away in front of their eyes.

"Oh Lord!! I can't believe this is happening here in our town. We need to hold a public meeting as soon as possible. We need to warn those who have property in the north end of town and surrounding areas," Robert said nervously.

"Absolutely. Let's get out of here and plan our strategy. We also need to talk to Ackerman and really try and convince him again with what's going to happen," Elise agreed.

The two families quickly went to the car and drove home in silence. Each one was thinking about what they just witnessed. Chief White Feather's words were swirling around in their brains and they were genuinely concerned for the town and the people and what the outcome was going to be. They couldn't even imagine it.

# CHAPTER SIXTEEN

THE WARRENS AND THE CHAPMANS called a meeting in the town hall for everyone to attend. It was in the paper and posters were hung up everywhere to encourage people to attend this meeting. They didn't let on what the details were but made it sound important. It was Wednesday morning and just about every family attended. Those who owned businesses closed shop for a couple of hours to be there and see what was happening.

The two families told the crowd what had been happening with the builder and what they observed in the woods with Chief White Feather. They had to choose their words carefully for fear that people wouldn't believe them.

"You're telling us that an Indian appeared before you in the woods? That's creepy!" A woman said in the audience.

"We wouldn't lie to you. It really happened. We didn't believe it either until we saw it with our own eyes," Elise said.

"I live in the north end of town. So what is supposed to happen to my home and my yarn shop?" another woman asked, concerned.

"I'm so sorry. The only thing I can tell you is to clear out of that home and shop and take anything with you that means something or has value. Tomorrow we're going to talk again with Ackerman and try and convince him to quit building. I don't know if it will do any good. We'll do everything possible to warn him," Meg reassured the lady and everyone else in the audience.

Some people believed what the families were saying about Chief White Feather, but some didn't. They really didn't understand what was happening and weren't experienced in the mystical aspects of life. It was a hard sell for some, but most of them listened and took to believing it and were thinking of ways to save their homes and existence in this town.

Sitting in the audience for the first time at a town meeting, was a Native American family, the Morningstars, who owned a jewelry store in the south end of town. The father was Jacob, the mother was Ramona. They had a son named Scout and a daughter named Shelly. After listening to people's pros and cons about the situation, the father of the family raised his hand to speak.

"Hello, Jacob. It's so good to see you and your family. Thank you for coming. What can I do for you?" Robert asked.

"We have been listening to everyone's remarks about this situation. May I make a suggestion to all of you? Believe what these families are saying. Use your gut feeling and think with your heart. There is powerful energy surrounding this earth and us as human beings. Anything is possible. I was talking with Ramona and we would like to accompany you to this meeting with the builder tomorrow. Maybe we can influence his decision to quit building. It would be very wise if he did," Jacob continued.

Everyone's heads turned to Jacob and they were listening with concern. Coming from a Native American that they all respected made them believe even more about what was happening to their town.

"That would be wonderful, Jacob. Thank you and your family for helping us in this matter. If Ackerman won't listen to you, I don't know who he will listen to. If he continues to build, we'll just have to protect the north end of town the best we can and hope it ends quickly," Elise said.

After the meeting, coffee and refreshments were served and a lot of talking was going on. Everyone was coming up to Jacob and his family to ask questions about the apparition of Chief White Feather and what it all meant. Jacob answered the best he could but recommended people ask the Chapmans and Warrens what they saw. They were there, Jacob and his family weren't. The Morningstar family knew of the traditions of the canoe journey and other lore with Native American history. They also knew how sacred the burial grounds were to the Native American and how building on them could be detrimental to the people living there.

People started leaving and were talking constantly as they were going out the door. The only ones left were the Chapmans, Warrens, and the Morningstars.

"We sure appreciate you helping us out on this, Jacob. I know you guys don't normally attend these meetings we have, but your gut feeling must have been working hard and you realized how important it was," Robert said.

Jacob and Ramona both laughed with Robert's remark.

"Well, you're right about that. I had a feeling it was about that building site. It's been bothering us all for quite a long time. Ackerman is getting himself in a lot of hot water, not to make a pun!" Jacob remarked.

They all laughed at Jacob's remark. They also agreed with him.

"We're going over to the site around 10 a.m. tomorrow morning. We'll meet there and hope he'll listen to us. I think it will make a good impression with you and your family there to support the town," Lottie said.

"We'll certainly do what we can to help. It's our heritage after all. We'll be at the canoe journey on Saturday, but we'll make sure our store is safe and our home and the surrounding areas," Ramona added.

"Thank goodness you guys are in the south end of the town. Isn't that weird? I don't know why it's only going to hit the North end of town," Meg commented.

"Actually, the spring and the woods are on the road at that end of the town and there's a definite slope coming from the spring following the path towards the town and beyond. The water will follow that slope and stay pretty much on that path. Water follows the least resistance and the slope will carry it out of the town and not in the heart of it. It's a blessing," Jacob informed.

"Thank you. That's reassuring to say the least. Well, thank you again and we'll see you in the morning," Elise said.

"We'll be there. Hold good thoughts. Goodnight folks," Jacob said.

# CHAPTER SEVENTEEN

IT WAS THURSDAY AND THE Warrens, Chapmans, and the Morningstars were on their way to the building site to talk with James Ackerman. It was two days before the Canoe Journey and the crisis Chief White Feather was warning the town about. They really needed to get through to Ackerman with the problems that lay ahead if building continued.

"Hello, is James Ackerman here on site? We urgently need to talk with him," Robert asked one of the builders near the Blake house.

"Uh, I think I saw him over there inspecting that building going up. Good luck!"

"That's an odd thing for him to say. It's almost as if they were expecting us," Elise commented.

As they walked towards the building where Ackerman was talking to one of the carpenters, there was tension in the air. Ackerman looked over at the families coming towards him, and continued talking to the man about what to do next with the design of the interior of the building. Finally he was through talking and turned to greet the families.

"Good morning. It's a beautiful day, isn't it?"

"Yes, it is. We need to talk to you, Mr. Ackerman. It's urgent. Can we sit somewhere and discuss the problems at hand?" Robert asked.

"Sure. Please call me James. No formalities here. Come over here to the trailer. There's plenty of seating in there. Would you care for some coffee?" Ackerman offered.

"No sir. We just need to talk," Elise answered.

They all took a seat in the trailer. Ackerman was acting like nothing was wrong and was ready for anything these families were going to give him. Surprisingly, Jacob Morningstar was the first to speak to Ackerman. He couldn't hold back any longer. He had something to say of importance.

"Mr. Ackerman, do you know anything about Indian tradition and lore? Do you have any interest or respect at all regarding our people?"

"I'm sorry, what is your name, sir?" Ackerman asked.

"My name is Jacob Morningstar, and this is my wife Ramona, and my children Scout and Shelly," Jacob answered.

"Mr. Morningstar, of course I do. I respect your people and ancestors. There's no question about it. What is the problem here?" Ackerman asked.

"You are building this mall on sacred land, Mr. Ackerman. This is an Indian burial ground, and there are bones, artifacts, and tools buried here. You are disrupting this whole site because of your greed," Jacob said bluntly.

"Now look here, Jacob, we're being careful not to disrupt anything on this land. This mall is important to the people of Blissville. It'll bring in revenue and tourists and…."

"Hold on, Ackerman. We didn't say we wanted this mall to be built. None of us did. You decided it needed to be done. You took advantage of Tyrone Blake when you bought it," Tom piped in.

"There are consequences to be endured if you continue to build here. You need to listen to what they are," Lottie added.

"Please. Don't fill my mind with all of that folklore mumbo jumbo. Nothing's going to happen if we build. Everything will go as planned," Ackerman tried to reassure them.

"No, it won't. It is only two days before the Canoe Journey lands on the beach at Port Bliss and at the same time that happens, there will be a great flood washing away what you have built here, and it will also take away part of the town of Blissville. You will have that on your conscience as well as ruins that will be left from your greed and stubbornness," Jacob warned.

"Okay, I've heard enough. I need you people to leave now and let me get back to work. I have a mall to build. Now, if you'll excuse me," Ackerman said as he was showing the families out the door of his trailer.

"What a stubborn and hostile man," Lottie said.

"You can say that again. We need to warn the town that he wouldn't listen to us. We need to prepare for the flood. The north end of town needs to be evacuated before Saturday," Robert said nervously.

They all came back to the Warren's house for coffee. They needed to discuss what just happened and what was going to happen in two days.

"On the morning of the Canoe Journey, my family and I will be at the festivities greeting the people and participating in the event," Jacob said.

"Yes, it's important for us to be there and greet our people. The children love it, and they need to know what the traditions are and what they stand for," Ramona added.

"We totally understand you guys. I wish we could be there to participate also. But I think we need to be here to make sure we don't lose anyone. Is your jewelry store safe from the flood?" Meg asked the Morningstars.

"Yes. We're on the south end of town and we have put anything of value in the safes and have brought some of the jewelry home with us. Can we do anything else to help you before all of this happens?" Jacob asked.

"No, I don't think so. You've been a great help to us today, Jacob. I wish that man had listened to you. If he survives this, he'll listen then, I'm sure," Robert said.

"Billy and Scotty, you've been so quiet through all of this," Elise realized.

"I just think it stinks. Why won't people listen? Why are they so stupid?" Scotty added.

"It's because they only think about money, Scotty," Billy said.

"Nicely said, Billy. Money rules in some people's minds," Tom interjected. "They don't think about the consequences of their actions. They have tunnel vision."

Scotty abruptly got up from the chair and ran into his bedroom on the verge of tears. He closed the door behind him and fell on his bed and sobbed.

"He's really upset, you guys," Meg observed.

"Yes, he is. After all, he was the one who saw Chief White Feather first. This all came to him before anyone else," Billy added.

"He's a sensitive boy. Would you mind if I talk to him before we leave?" Jacob asked.

"No, not at all, Jacob. Maybe you can ease his mind about it all," Robert answered.

Jacob walked to Scotty's room and gently rapped on his door. He heard a muffled sound.

"Who is it?" Scotty asked, sobbing.

"It's Jacob, Scotty. May I come in, son?"

"Yeah. The door's open."

When Jacob entered the room, he closed the door behind him and sat on the bed next to Scotty.

"Scotty, life and people can be very complex. It is all a learning experience. Mr. Ackerman will have a very big lesson to learn from all of this. I'm positive no one will be hurt in the flood on Saturday. There will be some damage, but it mostly will affect the building site. It must go and be washed away. It will probably wash away some of the remains of the burial site also, but the main reason is to be rid of it so that the land can be restored to the way nature meant it to be. Do you understand what I'm saying?" Jacob asked in a tender and loving way.

"Yes, I guess I do. I'm sorry for crying like a baby, but I think it all is such a mess. I don't want to see people hurt and their stores ruined. It doesn't have to be that way, but that stupid man won't listen. I'll be okay. Thanks for coming here to talk to me," Scotty said, giving Jacob a big hug.

Jacob was moved by Scotty's understanding and tenderness with the whole situation. Jacob left and Scotty remained in his room. He picked up a book he was reading and got lost in the plot of the story so he wouldn't have to think about the events of the day.

"Is everything okay?" Elise asked Jacob.

"Your son will be fine. He's a very sensitive and understanding boy. You've done well in bringing up your children, Elise," Jacob complimented both Elise and Robert.

"Thank you Jacob. You've done the same. In fact, I think we've all done well with our children. May God bless Blissville!" Robert said with enthusiasm.

With that, the Chapmans and the Morningstars left and the Warrens turned out the lights to get some much needed sleep.

# CHAPTER EIGHTEEN

I T WAS SATURDAY MORNING, AND the crowds were already forming at Port Bliss Beach waiting for the canoe journey event. The water was almost like glass, very still and calm. Once the tribes arrived they would have two days of celebration. Around 20 canoes from 9 to 12 tribes were expected to arrive in the early afternoon. They would be greeted by more than 200 people. Tents, awnings and coolers dotted the sand in anticipation. Each canoe would request permission to land and be welcomed.

People started gathering at the water's edge with hand drums to begin the ancient chants to welcome the first of the canoe journey tribes. A feeling of anticipation was filling the air as the arriving canoes' tribes raised their paddles in unison. The young men jumped overboard into the shallow bay water and began bringing the canoe up onto the shore, then the rocks, and with a final effort, up onto the sand safe from high tide. Each canoe and each paddle were hand carved with each tribe's colors, shapes, and artwork. Many of the canoe family members were young and they would learn and connect with their traditional culture.

Meanwhile, the people of Blissville were nervously anticipating the oncoming flood that would do away with the building site at the Blake estate. No one was working at the site on Saturday. The citizens had cleared out their stores so the merchandise wouldn't get damaged. During the night the bubbling spring had increased its water production tremendously.

"I wonder what's happening at the site?" Jacob remarked to his wife, Ramona. They were at Port Bliss enjoying the festivities of the canoe journey.

"I haven't heard anything. I told Elise to call me if anything major happened," Ramona answered.

The Chapmans and Warrens were together at the Warren's house pacing the floor and didn't know what to do with themselves. The kids wanted badly to go the spring but of course their parents wouldn't allow it. Flash floods can be very dangerous and come without much warning.

"I wish something would happen so it can be over with soon," Scotty commented.

"I know. I agree with you. This waiting is driving me crazy," Meg responded.

"Maybe it won't be that bad. Just a little scare or something," Billy said.

"I wonder if Chief White Feather is there at the spring," Scotty wondered.

"Well, if we could go there we could find out," Meg said, looking at her parents.

"Don't even think about it. We just stay here and see what happens," Robert advised.

At the building site water was starting to flood the end of the property nearest the Elkwa River. The spring was very active and saturating the area around it. Chief White Feather was there and waiting for the moment when the spring would let loose with full force. It was slow right now, but when the time was right it would do its damage.

During the first night of tribal celebrations, the tribes would be welcomed starting with those who had traveled the farthest, and then they would perform songs and dances of their culture. It was a very powerful event. Off in the distance a loud chant could be heard. Another canoe arrived to the shore. The spectators were snapping pictures up on the pier. "Come ashore and share our food and song" was said over and over as each boat was welcomed. With a final drum stroke the remaining canoes were brought out of the water and up to the waiting sand.

One final canoe was making its way to the shore. It was big and very decorative. It slowly paddled its way to meet the greeters. For some reason, unbeknownst to the people on the shore and the other tribes awaiting this canoe, it was taking its time and the atmosphere was suddenly quiet and anticipatory. Various people of the tribes were talking amongst themselves and wondering what was going on. The air was changing and there was a foreboding surrounding the activities.

At the building site, water was now gushing forth with strength and purpose. A roar from the water permeated the air around this sacred ground, and Chief White Feather was following the path of the water which was near the town of Blissville. The sound of limbs cracking off trees, and the roar of the water could be heard. The Chief was chanting in his native tongue, and praying to the Gods to spare most of the town. The people here were not responsible for this needless disruption of the ancient Indian burial ground. The water was finding the path of least resistance and flowed through one end of the town. The structures that were being built on the land were now a pile of wooden rubble. At the same time this was happening, the last canoe arrived on the shore for the journey event.

As the last canoe landed, many tribal members helped pull it up onto the shore. It was big and heavy and many people were paddling in it to arrive for this important event. Once they arrived and were greeted, the atmosphere around there went back to what it was before the flood did its damage miles away from Port Bliss Beach. The two events happened simultaneously. The tribes felt a heavy weight lifted and didn't consciously know why this was happening. They would certainly find out later on after the festivities.

Once the water from the flood accomplished what it set out to do, it stopped gushing forth from the spring, it was suddenly still, and soaking into the ground as much as it could, and Chief White Feather thanked the Gods for their understanding about ruining the town of Blissville. Minimal damage was done to the buildings in town. Some repairs would need to be done, but the wood left from the building site could be used for tribal purposes if Ackerman didn't take the wood for his own use. On the site the buildings weren't finished, only a shell of what it was going to be. The water knocked down what was there very quickly. The Blake house was not demolished. There was flood damage on the inside and around it but it could be repaired. However, the other structures were gone.

The Warrens and the Chapmans along with other families of the community were standing at the opposite end of the town where the flood was gushing forth. No one said a word but they were watching with their mouths agape at the strength of the water and where the water was flowing. It was almost as if someone were controlling the flow and causing as little damage as possible to the town and the shops. Of course, The Warrens and the Chapmans knew who that was. When the water subsided and all was fairly quiet, they all breathed a sigh of relief. Then by Monday morning, when Ackerman and his men came to continue with their building, a new set of problems would arise. They were not looking forward to it.

The Morningstars stayed a little while longer at the canoe journey festivities, but were anxious to get back to Blissville and find out what was happening. As they arrived into town, they were amazed that there wasn't a tremendous amount of damage, and they saw the Warrens and the Chapmans still standing there and talking about what had just happened.

"Well, as you can see there wasn't much damage to the shops and for that we're thankful," Robert said.

"I can see that. Have you gone to the building site yet?" Jacob asked.

"No, we were just about to go see. That is if we can get near the place," Elise added.

"I think we need to go see what damage has been done there as well. Come Monday morning we're going to have to contend with Ackerman and explain as best we can about what happened," Jacob warned.

All three families drove to the Blake property and could only get close enough to see that the buildings were demolished. They were glad to see that the Blake house was still standing.

"The job is done. After Ackerman comes here on Monday, I hope he will let the tribes take the wood that is left to help them in their own building to help their people. I wonder if he'll sell this land. He would be wise to do that," Jacob said with emotion.

"Let's hope that he does. He's lost this battle and he would be wise to go somewhere else to satisfy his hunger for money," Lottie commented.

"Wow, I can't believe how powerful that water was. It's amazing," Scotty said in awe.

"Yes it is, Scotty. Water is very powerful. I can't wait to go to the spring when the water subsides," Meg said with excitement.

"I agree. We'll have to wait a while though. It's looking pretty flooded from here. It feels as though a great weight has been lifted, doesn't it?" Billy asked.

"It sure does, Billy. This has been a miraculous experience. Jacob, how was the canoe journey event?" Robert asked.

"It was remarkable as always. A lot of tradition is involved. Curiously, the last canoe, which was very large, slowly came in to the shore and at that time the atmosphere around there was quiet and foreboding. No one could figure it out. I think it had something to do with events that were happening here. They were meant to work together. I don't even think the tribes knew what it was, and I doubt that the last canoe to arrive knew it either. Everyone will soon find out though. Nothing is by chance in this world, and we're all connected in one way or another," Jacob mused.

"I think you're right, brother. Thanks for your help in this matter and your wise input into what was happening. I think we need to have a town meeting tomorrow and talk about what has happened and find out how everyone is. All of you come back to the house and we'll get a list out and start calling," Robert suggested.

"Sounds good. I'll bring some pizzas over and we'll have a little dinner while we do it," Jacob answered.

"Thanks, Jacob. See you in a bit," Robert said.

They all got into their cars and drove over to the Warren's house. The Morningstars came a little later with pizzas, beer and some ice cream. They were all very hungry after a long day and the stress of all that happened.

During and after eating they all made phone calls on their cells to various families in Blissville and telling them about the meeting on Sunday around noon. They were all anxious to get together and decide what to do next.

"That was delicious. Thank you, guys, for bringing the food. I'm sorry it took this problem to get to know you and your family, Jacob. We need to do this more often," Robert said.

"I second that," Tom added.

"Absolutely. We all get along famously. It's been fun in a weird way. Do you know what I mean?" Lottie asked.

"I know exactly what you mean," Ramona answered.

"It's been an adventure to say the least. I mean how many people have the privilege to see and experience someone like Chief White Feather?" Meg added.

"Not many. That's for sure," Scotty said with a mouthful of pizza.

"It certainly has been a wild experience. I've been writing a diary since day one and I'm still going to write more after Monday. It'll be interesting to see how Ackerman takes this," Billy wondered.

"I'm afraid not very well, Billy. I was thinking. Tomorrow when we have the meeting let's suggest that a group of people go over to the site and confront Ackerman. There's power in large numbers," Jacob suggested.

"Excellent idea. He can't do much about it. I just hope he doesn't start building again on the land. I'm afraid of what would happen if he did," Robert surmised.

"I don't think he'll build again. I have a feeling he will try and sell the land to be rid of it. He's lost money on this venture of his," Jacob pointed out.

"Well, it's late and we need to get ourselves to the town hall for that meeting tomorrow. I'm anxious to talk to people and see how things are coming along," Lottie said.

"Thank you again Jacob and Ramona for the food and all your help," Elise said hugging them goodbye.

# Chapter Nineteen

C OFFEE AND REFRESHMENTS WERE BEING set up for the meeting in the town hall. Everyone showed up for this very important get together. They were chatting non-stop and the air was filled with excitement and relief at the same time.

"Quite a turnout for this meeting, don't you think?" Jacob asked Robert.

"Yes, but I'm not surprised. I was looking around outside before coming here and there seems to be little damage to the shops and trees in town. The water really did concentrate on the edge of town. It's almost as if the flood knew where to go and had a definite destination," Robert surmised.

"That's true my friend. Damage was done where it needed to be. It looks like everyone is here. I guess we can start in a few minutes," Jacob suggested.

"Elise, how did you sleep last night?" Lottie asked.

"Like a baby. I haven't slept that good or for that long in weeks. How about you?" Elise asked in return.

"Wonderfully. I'll sure be glad when this is all over for good. Tomorrow is kind of scary. I just hope that we see the last of Ackerman after he finds out what happened," Lottie commented.

"Okay, ladies and gentlemen. Please be seated and we'll get started on this important meeting. Thank you all for being here. It doesn't look like much damage was done to most of your businesses. That's a good thing," Robert said starting the meeting.

"A few young trees were knocked down at the edge of town where the water came gushing through. We were watching from the hill above town and it was something else to behold," Ken Martin said. He and his family owned the bakery in town.

"I can only imagine, Ken. Are there any other comments about the flood? Please feel free to tell us. We want to hear everything. Did any of you suffer any damage to your homes or businesses?" Robert asked.

"Well, my property is flooded still. It sort of washed away the vegetable garden and some of our rose bushes. But our house is intact," George Morley said. He was in direct line with the flood coming through town. However, his house was set back far enough that it didn't suffer any damage.

"My real estate office suffered some damage to the interior. We left the windows open to dry it out. But I'm afraid the smell will last a while," Karen Stein said. She and her family owned the real estate office in town and had been there for twenty years.

"I'm sorry to hear that Karen. Let us know if we can help. We're here to help anyone that needs it. We are a community who cares about each other. Don't forget that people. We own a hardware store and if there's anything we can get you to repair any damage let us know. In fact, write down what you need in the way of materials and repairs and we'll try and help you out," Robert offered.

There was a round of applause for Robert and his family for offering to help. It meant a lot.

"Are there anymore comments or damage reports from anyone? Tomorrow Ackerman comes back to continue building on his site. Or at least he thinks he is," Robert said. A round of laughter was heard after his comment.

"He has a surprise waiting for him and his crew," Elise added.

"I'd love to see his face when that happens," one of the townspeople commented.

"Well, what I'm about to ask all of you will allow that to happen. How many of you would be willing to come to the site with us and stand there in front of Ackerman and make sure he doesn't start building again? The more people who show up the more he will understand that we're a force to be reckoned with," Robert said.

A lot of hands went up and everyone loved the idea.

"Fantastic. Thank you everyone. We need to make sure that Ackerman doesn't start building again. Our friend Jacob has warned that if he does start, the consequences will be far worse than they are now. Isn't that right, Jacob?" Robert asked.

"Yes. This is serious. I think when Ackerman sees what damage has been done he will have to back off," Jacob added.

"What time do you want us to be there?" A member of the audience asked.

"If you could be there around noon that would be great. I can hardly wait to see his face when he realizes what has happened," Robert anticipated.

"That's for sure. Are there anymore comments?" Elise asked.

"Yes. Thank you for all that you're doing to save this town and the Blake property. You brought this whole thing to our attention and we didn't listen at first, but after what happened we have a whole new outlook on what can happen in life when it's necessary for preservation," Celia Colman added. Celia owned the Tea Spot Café in town.

"Here, here!!" Everyone added in response for what Celia commented on.

"Thank you everyone. There's plenty of coffee and refreshments left. Please enjoy and we'll see you tomorrow around noon," Robert finished.

Everyone was in a good mood and enjoying visiting with their friends. There was a lot of laughter and hugs.

Jacob was feeling quiet after the meeting and went outside to get some fresh air. He stood facing where the flood had been and said a silent prayer for his people and the land that was preserved after the event. As he prayed, he noticed a light shining at the edge of town. The light turned into a figure and he knew right away who it was. As Jacob looked at the figure before him, he nodded in respect and the figure of Chief White Feather nodded back. There was a definite connection at that moment. A connection only they could understand. As he stood there, Ramona and the kids came out and stood by him.

"Are you okay my husband?" Ramona asked.

"I'm just fine. Kids, let's say we go home now and get a good night's rest," Jacob said with a smile on his face. He felt certain that everything would work out as planned.

# CHAPTER TWENTY

I T WAS MONDAY MORNING AND Ackerman and his crew drove up to the site earlier than expected. Everyone got out of their car. Silence. Ackerman and five of his men slowly walk towards the site with their jaws dropped. They couldn't believe what they were witnessing. The ground was very wet and sloshy and there were remains of the three buildings they were in the process of erecting. They weren't prepared for this. They needed boots to be able to walk around and figure out the damage that was done.

"What in the name of God happened here?" Ackerman said with a hoarse throat. He could barely get the words out.

"I don't know boss, but I would say a major flood of some kind happened while we were away," Joe surmised. He was the foreman of the group of workers.

"Oh my God, I've lost money because of this disaster. What's that over there?" Ackerman asked.

"Uh, it looks like bones boss. Holy cow, I think this *is* an Indian burial ground after all," Mark said. He was another worker on the site.

"They tried to warn me about this. I didn't listen. Now look what's happened," Ackerman said.

Just as they were looking at the mess, more cars pulled up to the site. The Warrens, Chapmans, Morningstars, and other families were there to see Ackerman's reaction.

"Good morning, Ackerman," Robert said. He was the first to talk.

"There's nothing good about it," Ackerman answered.

"Can't say we didn't warn you," Jacob added.

"Rub it in why don't you? What the heck happened here?" Ackerman asked, hoping for a logical answer.

There were rumblings in the crowd of people that started forming.

"Take a look at the ground, Ackerman. Do you see anything? Any signs of life before you came here to destroy this burial ground?" Jacob asked.

There was silence. No one spoke. When everyone saw what the flood had washed up they were shocked. Heads were bowed down in embarrassment and shame.

"There are bones of my ancestors and also beads and artifacts that belonged to them. That's what you see. The great waters washed them up to show you what you've done to this land. If you have any conscience at all, you will give this land back to the people who deserve to have it. They will clean it up and preserve it and the house that sits over there," Jacob said, trying to convince Ackerman to do this.

Finally after much thought and consideration Ackerman gave in to the disaster before him. He knew in his heart that what Jacob was saying made sense. He didn't want to cause any more trouble than he had already. He turned to Jacob and made a deal with him.

"Jacob, I will sell this land and the house to you and your people for one dollar. I will bring the paperwork tomorrow morning. I'll meet you all here at 10 a.m. if that's okay with you," Ackerman offered.

Cheers rang through the crowd. Everyone applauded and hugged each other. Ackerman and his men stood there and realized what had just happened and were pleased with it all.

"Also, may I add. Thursday morning my men and I will be here and will help with this mess. We'll help you clean it up. We will have the proper boots to wear to muck our way through this ground. We will also help to bury the bones that were washed up and anything else that needs to be done. I hope you'll forgive me for this," Ackerman said with remorse.

"You're forgiven, brother, and thank you for your offer of this land and for the help," Jacob said.

"You came through, Ackerman and I thank you on behalf of everyone here," Robert added.

"Yes, thank you," Elise said shaking his hand.

Lottie and Tom came up to Ackerman and shook his hand also. In fact, various people came up to him and thanked him. The sun came out and shone brightly on the site and the birds started chirping for everyone to hear. It had been fairly quiet up until now. All was well.

"Whew, that was something else wasn't it?" Scotty said to Meg and Billy.

"Yeah, it sure was. I bet Chief White Feather's happy now that this has been resolved," Billy said.

"I want to go to the bubbling spring tomorrow and see how big it is. Maybe we can see the Chief while we're there," Meg suggested.

"Sounds like a good idea. That is if our parents will let us go," Billy wondered.

"Things are quieted down now. It shouldn't be a problem," Scotty added.

# CHAPTER TWENTY ONE

THE WARRENS, CHAPMANS, AND THE Morningstars hurried through their breakfasts to get over to the site to meet with Ackerman. They all arrived there promptly at 10 a.m. Excitement filled the air as the families waited for the paperwork to be handed over to Jacob and his people. Many of their friends joined in this joyous occasion. The tribal people would benefit having this land. Jacob was already planning on what to do with the house and the property. Some families didn't have homes and needed a place to stay and sleep. The house on the property, after being cleaned up after the flood, would accommodate several of those families. On the land itself, they would plant corn just as Blake did, and other vegetables and share with other families.

"Good morning. I'm glad to see you all here. Needless to say I'm ashamed of what happened here in the last few days. However, when I sell this land for one dollar to Jacob and his friends and family I think I will have redeemed myself, I hope. Jacob, will you sign on the dotted line please?" Ackerman asked, with a smile on his face.

"I would be honored," Jacob said with pride.

Everyone applauded at the signing of the deed to the property. After signing, Jacob reached into his pocket and pulled out a dollar bill and gave it to Ackerman. The people laughed and some were wiping tears from their eyes.

"On Thursday my men and I will be here to help you clean up this property and the house. I'm afraid there is some flood damage on the inside, especially on the first floor. What do you plan on doing with the house if I may ask?" Ackerman was curious.

"There are some families who don't have a permanent place to stay. We plan on giving them the space to call home. Also food will be planted on this land to nourish my people," Jacob answered.

"Wonderful. I'd love to see it when that happens. We'll be here on Thursday to help you with everything," Ackerman said.

"See you Thursday," Robert added.

Ackerman left.

"I'm so dumbfounded with everything that has happened after the flood. I honestly never thought Ackerman would do what he's done for the people," Elise commented.

"I didn't think so either. It's remarkable," Lottie added.

"He does have a conscience after all," Tom said sarcastically.

"I have to give him credit. He's lost a tremendous amount of money on this project. Sometimes you just can't read people and what they'll do in a crisis," Robert observed.

"I think seeing the bones and artifacts of the buried tribes had something to do with it," Jacob surmised.

"Absolutely. Who wouldn't react to something like that?" Elise asked.

"What happens to the bones that were washed up? Will they be buried again?" Scotty asked nervously.

"Yes son. They will be buried again. I feel there's a peace in the air now. Do you feel it? The Gods are happy and all is right with this sacred land," Jacob observed with emotion.

"Yes, I feel it too. I wonder what the spring area looks like," Billy asked.

"Good question. Speaking of the spring, Billy, Scotty, and I want to go there tomorrow. May we please check it out?" Meg asked her mom.

"I suppose so. The water should be soaked in pretty much by now. I would bring boots though just in case," Elise suggested.

"Thanks Mom. I wasn't sure you would let us go. We want to see if Chief White Feather is there and we're just curious what it looks like after the flood," Meg said.

"I can assure you he is happy now and relieved this is over. You may not even see him there at this time. He was there for a purpose and his job is done," Jacob stated.

"You have a point. But we want to see anyway. Maybe he will be there to say goodbye. I really like him. He's very cool," Scotty said.

Jacob chuckled at Scotty's reaction to the chief. He was thrilled that all the families involved had been so understanding and had shown sensitivity to the history of his people.

"Come over to our house guys, we have pasta and wine and would love to have you for lunch. I also made a salad early this morning figuring to share with you all," Elise offered.

"That sounds great. I'm starved. Can I bring ice cream? We'll stop off and get some," Lottie suggested.

"Yeah, let's bring some ice cream," Billy said.

"See you in a bit," Elise said.

# CHAPTER TWENTY TWO

"Get up sleepy head. We need to go to the spring. I can't wait," Scotty said to Meg who was sleeping in.

"Don't be impatient, Scotty. It was a hard day yesterday. Lots of stress. Pour the orange juice and fix some toast and I'll be ready soon," Meg reassured him.

Scotty got busy in the kitchen fixing their breakfast. He was being noisy. Elise woke up and looked at the clock and groaned while laying back down and going to sleep again. Robert mumbled about what was going on. Then rolled over and fell back to sleep.

A half an hour later Meg and Scotty were out the door. They picked up Billy and headed for the spring. They were keyed up and excited about what they might see. This whole event was surreal for them and everyone else in Blissville. They felt special that this happened here and that it was solved and taken care of without a lot of damage.

They drove up to the entrance to the hiking trail for their walk to the spring.

L.M. Henderson

"What a beautiful day," Meg observed.

As they walked through the mud, they noticed many broken twigs and damaged plants because of the power of the water that rushed through here. A few small trees were on the ground blocking the trail. They had to step over them as they walked. It flooded the whole area, not just the site where the building was taking place. They were getting closer to their spot with the bubbling spring.

"Here we are. At least we still have our rocks to sit on. Now it's really quiet here. No birds. That's weird," Scotty said.

"Not really, my son. The birds and wildlife know when I will be here," Chief White Feather said without being seen yet.

"Did you hear that?" Billy asked.

"Sure did. He's here but just not showing himself," Meg observed.

"Look guys. He's coming! I can see the mist that happens before he shows himself," Scotty said excitedly.

"I'm sure you all noticed there wasn't much damage to your town," Chief White Feather said with compassion in his voice.

"No there wasn't, Chief. Thank you. The damage was done where it was supposed to happen. Ackerman backed down and offered the land to the Morningstars for one dollar. Can you believe it?" Meg asked.

"Yes, I can. That man took a good hard look at the land after the flood and noticed the bones of our people and the damage that was done," Chief White Feather said with sadness.

"The land will be used for growing vegetables and the house will be used for shelter for several of the families that don't have a place to live," Meg told the Chief.

"He ended up being a good man after all. He found his heart. That's very important. I must go now my friends. Thank you for your help in resolving this dilemma for our people. You listened well and we are very proud of you over here. Be well and always lead with your heart and feel compassion for your fellow man," Chief White Feather said as he faded away.

Meg and Billy smiled and started to leave but noticed Scotty sitting on his rock with his head down, sobbing.

"Scotty, what's the matter? Are you okay?" Meg asked concerned.

"I don't want him to leave. I really like him a lot. We'll probably never see him again. I'm sad about that," Scotty said through his tears.

"Oh Scotty," Meg went over and hugged her brother with compassion.

As they were leaving Scotty noticed something on the ground. He bent down and was so excited he couldn't stand it.

"Look! Look! A white feather. He left a white feather. Thank you, Chief," Scotty said aloud.

On the way to the car Scotty couldn't stop looking at the feather. It was perfect and it meant so much to him. He would save it and cherish it always. His tears disappeared.

# CHAPTER TWENTY THREE

IT WAS CLEANING DAY AT the site. Ackerman was there with his men, and as many townspeople who could make it. Of course, the Warrens, Chapmans, and the Morningstars were there before anyone else. Jacob was the organizer and told the people what to do with the bones and any artifacts that were found. This was an important job for everyone to do. Jacob took this very seriously. He whistled to get everyone's attention.

"It's good to see all of you here today. We must dig holes to rebury the bones that you find. If you find any beads or anything else that belongs to the tribes bury them with the bones. Be gentle and consider in your heart what you are doing. This is sacred ground. Treat it as such, please. Thank you for your help today. If you have any questions please ask," Jacob said to everyone before they got started.

One could hear a pin drop it was so quiet. All you could hear was the shovels dig into the dirt as they buried the remains. The ground was muddy and easy to dig into.

Meg was digging and the shovel hit something. She bent down to check what it was. It was a blanket with something wrapped inside of it. As she slowly unwrapped the blanket, she jumped back and yelped. Tears were running down her cheeks.

"What is it Meg?" Elise asked.

"I don't know. I think it's a skeleton wrapped up. It isn't very big. I think it's a…." She couldn't finish what she was saying.

At that moment Jacob saw what was happening and quickly went over to Meg to see what she was so upset about.

"Look Jacob. Is that a child? I feel so bad," Meg said while sobbing.

"Yes it is. Probably around six years old. Her soul is safe, Meg. Don't worry. We will gently wrap her up and bury her again carefully. I'll take care of this and you work somewhere else, okay?" Jacob asked.

"Thanks Jacob," Meg left to work further away.

It took almost the whole day to rebury the bones of the tribal people and their belongings. It was quite an experience for everyone. Not much talking was going on because the people were touched and feeling sorry that the circumstances causing them to have to do this happened at all.

After it was all over with, Jacob thanked everyone that attended and helped.

"You have all been working so hard and I thank you from the heart for what you did here today. My tribal ancestors are pleased also and thank you. I wanted to tell you that I've decided to name this land White Feather Homestead. I thought it was very appropriate. Go home now and rest and think about what was accomplished today and know that you helped these souls to rest in peace once again," Jacob said to everyone with love in his heart.

As everyone was leaving they came over to Jacob and patted him on the shoulder, shook his hand, and thanked him for the experience of making things right again. They all the loved the name he chose for the property. Scotty was especially elated. He told Jacob about the white feather he found near the spring. It was a day no one in the town of Blissville would ever forget.

# CHAPTER TWENTY FOUR

I T WAS THE END OF summer and Meg had decided to work and help out in the family hardware store for a year before deciding which college to go to. She still wasn't sure. Scotty was back at school and was talking to everyone about the summer's excitement and experiences. He even brought his white feather to show people. They thought it was awesome.

Billy was back at school and working hard to earn a scholarship for college. He was smart and when he put his mind to work it served him well.

The Warrens were pleased to have Meg working with them in the store. She would tidy up and help customers and did just about everything that was needed.

Lottie Chapman was getting many catering jobs and loved doing it. Tom's lumber company was very busy and he had to hire more people. A building spike hit the town of Blissville and more retired people were coming up there to live. It was beautiful and serene and that was what people wanted.

As the sun started to set, a herd of elk were looking for a place to bed down for the night. That's what they do. Each day they roam around to find a suitable spot to rest. The head of the herd called everyone to gather around him with a high pitched yelp. They would slowly walk over to him. It was quite a sight.

This particular night, the herd of elk decided to bed down in White Feather Homestead. Also, two bald eagles flew into their nest in one of the giant cedar trees. Animals and birds loved this property and were seen many times coming to this sacred parcel of land to rest.